The NO BAD BOY Rule

RULE #2

ASHLEY ERIN

The No Bad Boy Rule
Copyright © 2015 by Ashley Erin

ISBN: 978-0-9939691-2-6

Cover Design by Kari Ayasha with Cover to Cover Designs
Model: Bryant Wood
Photographer: Eric Battershell
Editing by Jessica Grover and Missy Borucki
Interior Design: Integrity Formatting

Dedicated to

Lori & Kristi

You have no idea how much you ladies

mean to me.

I love you both.

CHAPTER 1

Ava

SQUINTING MY EYES to see through the heavily falling snow, I finally see the road to Parkland University. Slowing, I turn down the road, gritting my teeth when I feel the rear end of my car slide out. My car spins on the ice, my knuckles white as I grip the steering wheel. It's too late to correct my vehicle as I slide front first into a snow drift.

Sitting there visibly shaken, I let my heart slow down before attempting to get myself out of this mess. Like I wasn't already nervous enough my first day of university, spending more time with new people, spending more time with Dax . . .

Normally winter driving doesn't bother me, but the icy roads compounded with feeling nervous for today, I don't feel like myself.

Shifting my car into reverse, the dreaded squealing of my tires tells me I'm stuck. My head droops as I groan, thinking about how I will never hear the end of this from Lucas. *Didn't I tell you it was too slippery to drive to school today, Ava? Why haven't you bought winter tires yet, Ava?* I love him dearly, but, good lord, is he overprotective.

Breathing deep, I open my car door and step out into the swiftly falling snow. Pulling my hood up over my head, I examine my predicament. The front tires of my car are buried. Tears of frustration form and I fist my hands to stop them, crying won't help and I'm better than this.

Popping my trunk, I grab the shovel I always keep in there during the winter and start digging. I may not be able to make it to my first class, but I am determined to make it to my second.

This is my fresh start. A chance to have a career that will allow me to provide the best life possible for Noah. He deserves to have all the chances I was given, and I know I need to find a lucrative career to do that.

I used to dream of painting all over the world. Studying at different universities, immersing myself in the culture of foreign lands. That dream faded when those two pink lines showed up.

Despite losing out on the luxury of a life spent painting and moving place to place, when I think of Noah there are no regrets. Breathing in the icy air, I lean on my shovel and gaze around me.

The world is silent, the beauty of the snow hiding its dangers. Spruce trees droop under its weight and everything is blanketed in glistening white. By the looks of it, I'm one of the few people entering or leaving campus today, there are no fresh tracks on the road.

Wind gusts, freezing my cheeks. The snow begins to fall even heavier, reducing visibility to less than ten feet. Thankfully, I planned to stay the night; I don't think I'm going anywhere until this blizzard is over. Sighing, I straighten my shoulders and start shoveling snow.

The snow is wet and heavy, and it doesn't take long for me to start sweating as I attempt to dig a clear path for my car. Underneath the snow is a thick layer of ice.

The sound of a vehicle turning off the highway draws my attention. Turning I wait until they're in view and I'm relieved when I recognize Andie's SUV. I wave when she pulls to the side of the road, my smile freezing as Dax gets out of the vehicle and not Andie.

Ever since he stormed into Lucas' apartment, he has been the star of several dreams I could never tell anyone about. He is a walking, talking fantasy and I am going to be spending two classes a week with him.

Gulping as I realize I've been checking him out, I shake my body slightly and meet his eyes. Those eyes that seem to read my mind, piercing right into my soul and devouring my deepest, darkest secrets.

He doesn't say anything as he walks over to me, his intense hazel gaze focuses on me before examining my hack job of digging my car out. I've only managed to uncover one wheel. Barely.

He turns back to me, the silence making me uncomfortable. Gulping, I look away from his gaze. "Hi, Dax. My car is stuck." *Seriously? Obviously you're stuck. What do you think he thought? That you were taking a leisurely stroll with a shovel?* "I mean . . . Obviously, I'm stuck. I'm just trying to dig myself out, but I think I might need to call a tow truck." *Shut up, seriously, just stop talking.* If I'm not mistaken, his lips twitch fighting a smirk, and I die a little bit. If the ground wasn't frozen, I would just start digging a hole to bury myself.

"Why don't I give you a ride to campus and you can call a tow truck from the warmth of Lucas's apartment?" His deep voice makes me jump. I love the way it sounds, a little rumbly but soft and low. Nodding in relief that he has finally spoken, I allow him to take the shovel from my hand. I stand there gaping at him as he puts it in my trunk, turns my car off, and grabs my bags from the back seat. "Coming?"

He chuckles as I scramble into Andie's SUV and I'm grateful I don't blush easily. I've only been around Dax a few times, but we've never been alone. Clearly being in his presence turns me into a stupid swooning girl.

The SUV is warm, and I gratefully tug my gloves off, flexing my fingers to work out the cold. Dax doesn't say anything as he shifts the car into gear, and I'm jealous when it moves effortlessly over the snow. Obviously, my brain cannot connect with my mouth properly, so I wait for him to say something, anything to fill the silence.

He doesn't.

I have this incessant need to fill awkward silences, and being in the vehicle with Dax, alone, has my brain working overtime. Swallowing all of the stupid things I might say, I angle my body towards the window. If I see him look at me, who knows what might spill out from the part of my brain that doesn't know when to shut up.

My body starts to thaw out and with Dax being outside my line of sight, my thoughts turn to Noah. Today is the first day I haven't driven him to pre-school since he started in the fall. It was more difficult than I thought it would be, kissing him while he slept before leaving. The discovery that I was pregnant five years ago made me think my life was over, now he is my life and I couldn't imagine him not being a part of it.

"Amazing, isn't it?" The sound of Dax's voice, soft and deep, jolts me out of my thoughts, and I'm surprised to see we have arrived at the apartment building that will be my home two nights a week.

"What is?" Was he talking to me and I completely missed it? That would be so rude.

"How difficult it is to leave him behind. Even if it is only for a few days." He looks at me empathetically, and my stomach feels like it flips over as we stare at each other.

"How did you know I was thinking about Noah?" Shock colors my voice and my throat feels raw with emotion.

"I've seen the kind of mom you are. Your world revolves around that little boy, as it should. To me, it seems obvious that's where your thoughts would be." He exits the car, leaving me gaping after him in awe.

Scrambling to follow him, I grab my bags and hurry into the building. "Today is the first time I haven't driven him to school. I guess I feel guilty, like by being here I'm putting my needs before his."

Dax falls into step beside me as we climb the stairs. "Hmph."

Glancing at him sideways as he grunts, I try to bite my tongue and not say anything stupid. "If I get a degree and find a good job, I can provide everything he could ever need. It's not selfish." My tone is defensive, and if I could get away with it, I would smack my head into the wall.

"Where the hell did you get the idea it was selfish?"

"You hmphed." His lips twitch as I mimic his grunt, he still hasn't actually smiled. Now that I think about it, I've only ever seen the smallest of smiles in the brief times we've been around each other. Most of the time he has this look of intense focus, as if he's critically observing every single thing around him.

"So? I was trying not to be a dick and call you an idiot for feeling guilty." The small smile peeks out before it's gone again in an instant.

"Oh." *You are an idiot.* I used to be more coherent around attractive guys. It got me into a lot of trouble, case in point: Joe. Apparently talking to guys and not sounding like a dumbass is a skill you can lose.

More awkward silence. "So, math class this afternoon." *Kill me now. Ava, you are almost twenty-one years old, not sixteen. Get your shit together.*

Dax looks at me, humor shining in his eyes as he fights a laugh. We finally reach the top floor and I rest my hand on Lucas's doorknob. Opening my mouth, I shake my head and turn towards the door clamping my lips together tightly. I give up. I can try again this afternoon.

"So . . . math class this afternoon," Dax says with laughter in his voice as he mocks me. Turning, I try to glare at him, but this time his smile is real. A heart-stopping smirk that pulls the corners of my lips up. "It's my only class on Tuesdays and Thursdays. I was going to grab a coffee on my way, do you want anything?"

His offer surprises me, and I can feel my jaw opening and closing like a fish. *Say something.* "A chai latte, please."

"Done. Save me a seat." He walks into the apartment he shares with Andie and shuts the door. Sighing in relief that I have time to gather my wits before I have to spend almost two hours with him, I wonder how the hell I'm going to keep my inappropriate thoughts in check.

Slipping in the door, I peek my head into the living room when I hear my brother's voice.

"Oh my God!" Slamming my hands over my eyes, I try to block out the image of Lucas and Andie half-naked on the couch as I back out of the room, colliding with the wall. "I have to sleep on there!"

Andie giggles uncomfortably as I hear Lucas swear. "I thought you had class?"

"I got stuck in a snow drift; class is halfway over by now. Seriously though, how am I supposed to sleep on there now that I've seen that?"

"I'm so sorry, Ava. You can uncover your eyes now." Slowly dropping my hands, I cautiously step back into the room. Andie stands in the middle of the room, blushing, next to Lucas who appears disturbingly chill about what just happened.

"I picked up your bed yesterday so you wouldn't have to sleep on the couch. Besides, it's not like we were having sex."

I can feel the look of disgust on my face. "It was bad enough."

"Lucas!" Andie scolds Lucas with a grimace. "Did you get your car unstuck?"

"No, I'm going to call a tow truck. Dax pulled up and gave me a ride." I adore Andie. Once you get to know her, she's sweet and caring. Admittedly, when I first met her, she scared the shit out of me. I've never seen someone who can look quite as mean as she can, except maybe her brother.

"Did you have your shovel?" Resisting the urge to roll my eyes, I nod. "Was your phone fully charged?" Sighing on another nod, I wait for Lucas to start lecturing me once again on how to get out of a slide, but instead he walks over and hugs me.

"Good."

I gape at him as he leads Andie into his room. Well, that's a change.

Giggling erupts from behind his closed door, and I hurry to my room and shut myself in, relieved that it blocks out the sounds that will inevitably come from Lucas and Andie. That's going to take some getting used to.

Glancing at the time on my phone, I face plant onto the bed Lucas has set up and close my eyes. My career as a college student has officially started. It almost feels too mainstream for me; it's going to be great.

Dax

LAYING BACK ON my bed, the stain in the ceiling shaped like a dick catches my eye. Some things can't be unseen. Maybe if I stick a poster over the top of it; that would be better than waking up to that every morning. Andie thinks it's hilarious, and whenever I start to forget it, she points it out.

Rolling over so my eyes aren't drawn in that direction, I contemplate how to pass the time until class. I hate sitting still and doing nothing. I play so many video games because it takes up space in my brain that fills with thoughts I don't want to have in moments like this.

Exhaustion makes my body feel heavy; maybe I can have a quick nap.

Setting my alarm, I close my eyes.

I'm beat and the day isn't even over yet. At least my final debt to Ivan has been paid. Technically, I wasn't supposed to be doing anything for him, but I committed to this job and to stay in his "good" graces, I followed through. Of course, he made me drive all the way to Edmonton last night to deliver it. No PayPal or e-transfer for him. Nope, he likes to do things face-to-face. More intimidation power.

Too bad for him I'm not easily intimidated. I'm bigger than he is, and I managed to gain clout within the organization of his gang while I was working for him.

His offer to reinstate me back into the Vipers holds no appeal. Walking away was one of the hardest things I've done, made easier only because I had no choice. My job was easy, I was good at it. I would be lying if I didn't admit at one point I thought of going back, despite the risks, the first time he tried to convince me I made a mistake. Saying no this time was one of the easiest decisions I've ever made.

Since starting Parkland in September, I finally feel part of something respectable. There is no way I'm going to blow it. My only regret is not taking Peyton with me when I left. She is too young to be part of that lifestyle and the thought of not being there to protect her makes me want to call Ivan to negotiate a deal.

I won't. She knows how to reach me if she needs my help. I just wish I could have seen her, made sure she was okay.

Guilt over not checking in on Peyton threatens to consume me. Another promise broken to another person I care about.

This is why I need to focus on staying within my new reality. Focus on a new life. A life I can be proud of. No more broken promises, no more failure.

Bunching my pillow, I clear my mind of this train of thought. Almost immediately, a pair of brilliant blue eyes fills in the space I've just vacated. Rescuing Ava was the distraction I needed after being alone with my thoughts and self-loathing for four hours.

She made me laugh when I was in a miserable mood, not an easy feat. Granted, she wasn't doing it on purpose, which made it even better. She was so adorably awkward. It is refreshing to see someone that attractive not be full of themselves or overly self-assured.

Being around Ava is a breath of fresh air. She's so innocent in comparison to every other girl I've been around. She draws out genuine smiles and makes me forget what I've done, even for a little while.

Focusing on having that reprieve in just a couple of hours, I finally feel myself start to doze off.

My eyes search the classroom for Ava. She hasn't arrived yet so I grab two seats in the back of the class, setting her latte on one of the desks to save her spot. Pulling out my phone, I realize I can't even text her because I don't know her number.

Loading *Plants vs. Zombie's*, I decide to occupy myself until class starts.

My neck tingles as I feel someone watching me. Continuing to play my game, I am aware of a body walking down the aisle, eyes on me.

It's hard to explain how I can tell when someone is watching me, but it's a gift and a curse. Sometimes I wish I could be blissfully ignorant like most of the people surrounding me. Who knows what they've been through, but I would be willing to bet that most of them would shit their pants if they knew the things I've seen and done.

The chair next to me slides out, and I finally look up to smile at Ava. She makes it easy to smile.

My lips fall into a frown when I see it's not Ava. The woman who is eyeing me up is slender and attractive; I'm also pretty sure I could bend her over this desk and fuck her in front of everyone. Too easy. Besides, I'm not about to give away Ava's seat just because some hot chick makes eyes at me.

"That seat is taken." Turning back to my game, I ignore the indignant noises she makes as she moves her ass out of Ava's seat.

Not long after the chick leaves, I can't even remember what she looks like anymore, I feel someone else sit in that seat. Scowling, I look up from destroying zombies, ready to rip a new one into whoever doesn't understand the coffee cup is indicating that seat is taken.

Ava's blue eyes widen as she takes in my expression, the movement of her throat drawing my eyes as she swallows nervously. "Did the zombies win?" Her question shocks a laugh out of me as I glance down at my game.

"No. I was kicking ass like I always do."

"Unless Andie plays." She smirks when she points out my sister's irritating ability to kick my ass at almost any game she plays. Shutting down my phone, I watch Ava get settled in her desk. This girl is different from the one I picked up off the side of the road. She seems more confident and sure of herself. Less flustered. I guess that makes sense, she did crash her car. Not exactly the best way to start your day.

Awkward Ava is funny and adorable. I'm curious what I will think of this side of Ava.

"She had to learn those skills from someone." Tucking my phone away, I'm disappointed when the professor comes into the room.

"Thanks for the coffee." She's leaning towards me, trying not to draw the professor's attention. She straightens in her seat as the professor starts talking. The fruity scent of her shampoo lingering.

Glancing as she stretches in her seat, I'm drawn to the way her body curves in all the right places. Leaning back in my chair, I shut that thought down immediately.

"I'm Professor Williams, and as you hopefully already know, this is Math 209." Williams rambles on about linear equations, functions, matrices and other things I'm sure will make me regret signing up for this course. It's all boring and predictable.

"Is it just me, or is he speaking a foreign language?" Ava's whisper makes me grin.

"Are you reading my mind? I was just thinking that I am already regretting signing up for this class." She laughs quietly, trying not to disrupt the professor's lengthy overview of the syllabus. The sound is breathy and intoxicating. I haven't heard Ava laugh often and I definitely want to hear it more.

"Seriously? Who signs up for a math class when they haven't been in school for almost three years? I should have taken some easy introductory courses." She grumbles.

"Try almost four years and you graduated high school with a baby, you're probably a secret genius. Just so you know, if you see me looking over at you during tests it's not because I'm cheating, I swear." Winking at her, I smile when she quietly laughs again.

Glancing around the room, I see everyone is taking notes. Tuning into what Professor Williams is saying, I groan when I realize I've missed some of his lecture. "Shit."

Ava smiles and gestures to her notebook. "I've got it."

"Damn and I always pride myself on how observant I am." Turning to a clean page, I focus in on the rest of the lecture.

Ava is going to be a distraction, one I don't need.

CHAPTER 2

Ava

"HELLO, SUNSHINE." DAX sits down at his desk, handing me a coffee. "How are you?" It's only the second week of class, and we have already settled into a routine, I've never looked forward to a math class this much before.

"Thanks for the coffee." Breathing in the tantalizing smell of whatever he's surprised me with today, I take a sip. The sweetness of caramel teases my taste buds and I close my eyes to savor the flavor. "I'm doing okay. Noah had a tantrum this morning when I was leaving. He wanted me to drive him to school. It sucked."

"That must be tough. I'm sure he will get used to it and it will get easier." Dax looks at me empathetically and to my mortification, I feel tears start to well.

"Things with him will get easier, Joe not so much. He's decided he wants to be more involved since I'm going to school and not doing my job. Four years he's been absent. Seriously? He thinks he has a right to judge me? I'm not going to keep him from Noah, but his judgment is hard to swallow." Recalling the argument we had this morning, the tears disappear as my earlier anger resurfaces. "It's completely ridiculous, but I don't want to talk about that asshole. How are you?"

"You know. Same as always." Grunting at his vague response, I can't understand how someone who takes such an active interest in how I'm doing has so little to say about himself.

"You are quite the conversationalist. I'm truly fascinated." My remark surprises me, and I realize that some of the awkwardness I felt at first is long gone. He's easy to be around, and I'm no longer a nervous wreck.

Dax's expression makes me choke on my latte, his jaw dropped in surprise. "Well, it's true. I don't know what 'same as always' is. Friendship is a two-way street, you know. I don't think it would kill you to talk about yourself once in a while."

"It might . . ." He sighs when I pointedly turn my body towards him and stare at him expectantly. "Honestly, I'm just boring. I go to class, hit the gym, and play video games. Occasionally the guys and I go out. I like boring, I have never had boring until I moved here."

"What do you mean, you've never had boring?" Andie and Dax are near silent when it comes to their past, and I've been curious since I met him about what gave him the hard edge that pushes people away.

"Nothing. It's not important anymore, and you don't want to know. Seriously, I have not always been the charming and delightful person before you today. I'm not a nice person." His gaze closes off, despite the forced smile on his lips and I see the relief in his eyes when Professor Williams walks into the classroom, already lecturing before he gets to the podium.

"I think you're a nice person." Picking up my pen, I tune him out and try to grasp the concepts we are being tested on next class. I want to smack him upside the head. This isn't the first time he's said something like this, yet there is not any evidence in his actions. The way he presents himself, the vibe he gives off, well that's a different story.

"You see what I want you to see." My head swings over on its own volition, his profile staring at his paper as he writes. Tension rolls off his body and I don't understand why my

14

comment has upset him, but something inside me tells me to shut my mouth.

I'm not good at listening to my internal common sense.

"Do people actually say shit like that? You may think that's true, but I guarantee that there are people who see through the act. Now shush, I'm trying to learn." He stares at me incredulously, and I bite my cheek to keep from laughing. Screw being awkward, I'm going to be me, and I grew up with a pain in the ass brother, I know how to dish it out.

An hour later, Williams finally stops lecturing and I have my belongings in my arms and the classroom behind me before Dax is even out of his seat. It bothers me that he is so closed off and it shouldn't. Sure, we're friends I guess, but that doesn't automatically give me a pass into the depths of his psyche. I just can't help but want to know more. Sighing as I squeeze past a group of people crowding the door to my next lecture, I know the fact that Dax is a mystery makes him more attractive to me. I'm hoping once the mystery is uncovered I can get back to life as it was before I met him.

"Someone looks like they are thinking a little too hard. Is that smoke coming from your ears? I thought I smelled burning." Shaking my head as Dean sits next to me, I turn to my brother's best friend. Most girls can't stand him because of how he talks about our gender, but I know the Dean behind the act.

"I'm pretty sure that smell is your giant ego deflating because you're stuck retaking a first year course." Sticking my tongue out at him when he winks at me, I see him glance at a blonde chick near the front of the room. "Latest conquest?"

"You know better." He smiles at the girl when she turns around, looking between us. "Her name is Morgan. I've been asking her out, and she finally said yes."

Smiling gently at him, I know how big of a deal this is. "Just make sure you remember to take care of yourself."

He groans good-naturedly and flips open his book. Shaking my head, I glance back at Morgan. Everyone says you shouldn't

judge someone by how they look and they're right, but I can't help analyze her. Dean struggles more than even Lucas knows. He's finally almost back to normal since Nina. I don't want to see him lose himself again.

Shutting the door, I stand in the entryway listening carefully. It sounds like they are playing a video game, but I've been fooled before. Andie and Lucas seem to forget that I now live here part time. "Is everyone decent?"

"Stop being dramatic and get in here." Someone mutters something that I can't quite hear, and Lucas laughs. Stumbling into the room before more jokes can be made at my expense, I almost fall flat on my face when Dax's smirk greets me. "Careful there, sis, remember to lift your feet."

Giving Lucas the finger, I plop myself between the guys and pull my legs underneath me. Absentmindedly, I start picking at the paint around my nails while staring at the TV. My thoughts flit between all of the things I need to get done before going home until they finally settle on Dax. He seems to fill my head frequently since he rescued me. We've shared just three classes and seen each other in passing a handful of times, yet he's managed to suck me in. I hate this addiction I have to guys who are mysterious. Bad boys are my weakness and Dax makes any previous guy I've been attracted to look like a saint.

Andie has mentioned that Dax has this magnetism about him, a draw that prevents you from being able to stay mad at him or hold him accountable for bad behavior. I can feel what she means. When he speaks, even if it's just to me, the people around us listen. He is someone I want in my life. The type of person who would be a great friend, but I know I need to keep a careful check on my feelings. He would be easy for me to fall for, fast and hard.

Zoning back in on the game and the guy's pathetic smack talk, I feel my eyes grow heavy. I'm too lazy to get up and go to my room, so I wiggle into a comfortable position between them and close my eyes. I can sleep pretty much anywhere and the noise they are making lulls me into dreamland.

My cell phone ringing startles me awake. I'm leaning on Dax's shoulder; the scent of his cologne surrounds me. Bolting into an upright position, I fumble around for my phone.

The sigh that escapes my lips as I see Joe's name on the screen is unavoidable, as is the audible groan. Rubbing my temples, I answer the call before my voicemail picks up. "Hello."

"We need to finish our conversation from this morning." His voice grinds on my nerves and the throbbing starts in my temple. What did I ever see in this man?

"I'm pretty sure we did finish it." My tone is cold and hard. It has taken years, but I've finally gotten to the point where he no longer can make me cry. The final straw was when Noah was in the hospital with pneumonia, and he didn't even come visit. "You clearly expressed that you think I'm selfish and demanded time with Noah, in a very unreasonable manner, might I add."

"Ava . . ." He sounds frustrated, and I admit that it gives me the slightest bit of pleasure.

"Joe . . ." Mimicking him, I roll my eyes as he sighs. I know I need to work with him, it's in the best interest of Noah, but I'm not going to make this easy. He has a lot of catching up to do. "What do you want?"

"I apologize for calling you selfish. It's been pointed out to me that I have no right to say that, but I want you to cooperate and let me be more active in Noah's life." The sound of a woman's voice comes over the speaker, and I barely choke back the laugh threatening to burst forth. Of course, a woman. This explains a lot.

Standing, I pace into the kitchen and back out ignoring the two sets of eyes following me. "It *was* ironic."

"I was thinking when you're in school Noah can stay with me." His tone is calm, drastically different from this morning.

Even though his request is outrageous, I respond in the same neutral tone. "No, absolutely not."

"Ava, don't be unreasonable."

"I'm not. Joe, you have seen Noah less than once a month since he was born. He's not spending three days a week with you. Besides, he's in pre-school and doing well." Breathing in deeply, I control my tone as much as possible, trying to keep it level and calm.

"You're right. What do you suggest?" Halting in my tracks, his tone surprises me. He sounds surprisingly sincere and vulnerable. What the fuck has changed in him over the past six months? Hell, from this morning.

"Oh. Well, we need to build up visits. He doesn't really know you.   I have told you for almost five years I won't keep him from you, but you need to deal with my terms." Peeling paint off a nail, I wait for him to process what I'm saying before I continue. "Let's start off with short visits, for which I will be present and see where it goes."

"Okay, Ava. I understand." He sounds disappointed and I push back the irritation I feel at myself for feeling guilty about it.

"This needs to be consistent. You can't start being in his life and then disappear. It's not fair to him." Not that I need to justify my reasons since he gave up his custody rights. Reminding myself this is in Noah's best interest, I try to be okay with this turn of events. In reality, it's spun me off my axis, and I'm flailing trying to understand how he can go from yelling at me to trying to compromise with me in less than twelve hours.

"Thank you, Ava." Hanging up on the promise I will text him dates to meet, I'm baffled at the change. Staring at my phone, I walk to my room ignoring the questions from Lucas.

Gently closing the door, I pull a fresh canvas from my closet and set it on my easel. I need to process that entire conversation and painting always helps me think clearly.

Dax

LUCAS STOPS THE game and stands to stretch, glancing in the direction of Ava's room. She's been in there for forty-five minutes. I shouldn't be keeping track, but I am. "Should she be alone right now?" I know enough of her history with Joe to recognize him wanting more access to Noah won't be easy for her. That conversation seemed to go well compared to previous ones she has mentioned and the look on her face when she left the room wasn't anger or sadness . . . It was bewilderment.

"She's in there coping. She doesn't let him upset her as much anymore, unless he pisses her off. She wasn't mad, though." I want to tell him that I know she's not mad, but I hold back. Instead, I nod and pick up my phone, rolling my eyes at a text message from Ivan. Deleting it without opening it, I get up and go to the kitchen needing something to do. Lucas looks up from his phone with a goofy grin. "I'm going to head out. Andie's done with class, and we want to go for a hike."

Leaning against the counter, I wait until Lucas closes the door. It's barely clicked before I'm moving down the hall to Ava's room. Knocking, I wait but silence greets me. Quietly turning the knob, I peek my head in the door.

Ava's back faces me, her hips shaking as she dances to whatever music is playing in her earbuds. A paintbrush in hand, she swipes it across the colorful canvas her body is partially blocking. Laughing as she does a little shimmy and spin, my body shakes with laughter as she stumbles upon seeing me. The paintbrush goes flying as she yelps and in between gasps for air, I manage to catch it.

"Well, that's embarrassing." Ava pulls her earbuds from her

ears. "What are you doing in here?"

Glancing around, I take in the simplicity of her room. She has some photos in frames on the dresser and a stack of blank canvases leaning against the wall. Aside from that, there are few personal touches to the room she calls home two nights a week. "I wanted to make sure you are okay." Leaning against the doorframe, I take a moment to look her over. She doesn't seem upset.

"Surprisingly, yes. As far as conversations with Joe go, that one was pleasant." She crosses the room and takes the paintbrush from me, rinsing it off in a cup of water she has on her nightstand. "I feel like I'm able to handle whatever Joe throws my way now. That wasn't always the case, there just came a time when I realized I was the one allowing him to upset me. I can only hope that his cooperative manner continues. It might not, so I'm going to enjoy it while I can. Plus, I know it's in Noah's best interest to have a relationship with his father, so this is a good thing. Although, if I'm honest, the idea of him being more active in my life makes me uncomfortable."

She dips her paintbrush into a vibrant orange, pursing her lips as she turns back to the canvas resting on a paint-splattered easel. Glancing at the floor, I grin as I see paint on her bare feet. How does that happen?

Stepping across the room, I peek over her shoulder, taking in the swirling colors that make up a beautiful sunset over water. Wow, I knew she was a good painter, but I had no idea she was this talented.

The sound of her brush strokes is the only sound in the room so I grab a seat on the floor, listening as she works. It's relaxing.

"It is a good thing, right? I mean, Noah should have a chance to know his father. And he could have changed. I know we argue a lot, but maybe that's my defense mechanism. People change, don't they?" She doesn't look at me and continues to swirl paint together.

"People can change. Maybe he has finally grown up." She nods and silence fills the room again. I keep telling myself that people can change because that's what I'm trying to do, and I hope for her sake that Joe isn't playing her.

Ava glances at me over her shoulder, turning quickly back to her painting when she sees my smirk. It hasn't taken long for me to realize that Ava can't handle long silences. Whenever we are together, I will purposefully be quiet just to hear what she has to say.

She changes brushes to one that looks like a fan; her lips are twitching with her urge to say something. Folding my hands, I hold my composure when she glances at me again, the hope in her eyes that I might be the one to break the stillness in the room. I wonder why she can't handle long periods of quiet. It's not that she needs to be the one talking, but whenever she is around anyone, she has this need to make sure there is conversation occurring.

"Before I found out I was pregnant, I wanted to be a painter. Travel the world, selling my art in markets all over. Never worrying about how much money I had because I was doing what I loved." She looks at the photo of Noah on her dresser and smiles. "Take classes in all of the great cities."

She looks so wistful. Whatever memories that are crossing her mind are obviously ones she's spent a lot of time thinking about.

"At the time, I was so bitter. I spent my whole pregnancy being angry and resentful. Then I held him in my arms." Her hand pauses over the canvas, head tilted to the side examining her work. "I thought people were full of shit when they said a child steals your whole heart. They're not. One look into the blue eyes that matched my own and he owned me."

She dips a brush into her black paint, adding white to create a soft grey. It's fascinating and therapeutic to watch her. Staying silent, I wait for her to continue speaking. Whatever is causing her to open up, I don't want her to stop.

"Every choice I make, every thought I have . . . It all has to do with ways to make his life good. That's why I was so mad when Joe called me selfish. The thing is, I want to be selfish sometimes. I want to do something that is for me and only me." Ava steps back from the canvas and examines it. My view is blocked from my position on the floor and I'm curious how much has changed since we've been talking.

She moves away from the canvas gathering her brushes and water cup, leaving me in her room to stare in awe at the masterpiece she has created.

The water looks like it's from a photograph and the vibrant colors of the sunset take my breath away. With my eyes glued to the painting, I feel Ava staring at me as she re-enters the room.

"Ava, I know that you love your son and all the sacrifices are worth it because you have him, but the art world needs someone of your talent. This. This right here is your something for you. You need to find a way, anyway, to get your work out there. You never know." Standing, I pop my knuckles and walk over to where she is gaping at me. "I need to go. See you Thursday."

Exiting her room, my hand is on the knob when I hear her walk quickly down the hall.

"I told you, you're a nice person. Only a wonderful friend would say something like that." Ava rests her hand on my arm. "Thank you, Dax. You have given me more with those words than you can understand. I'm lucky to have a friend like you."

Giving her a small smile, I pat her arm. "I call it like I see it."

Closing the door behind me, I pause. She doesn't understand what being around her does for me. She makes me feel like I'm not a horrible person. She talks to me like she would anyone else. I'm certain that will change the moment she finds out who I truly am, who I'm trying hard not to be. Even if I wasn't required to change, being around her makes me want to.

I could have stayed in her room, listening to her paint and talk. That's risky. Being her friend, it's not something I want. I don't think it's possible for me to be friends with Ava. Something more seems to be there. A flame that brightens the darkness in my head, no one has done that for me before. She is more. I don't deserve more . . . not yet.

CHAPTER 3

Ava

PULLING THE BED Lucas made for Noah out from under mine, I shift my room around so there is a path to walk. Lucas invited us for a sleepover, and since the roads have improved significantly, I decided it was a good idea. Mom and Dad need a break, and I need quality Noah time.

School has been eating up more time than I had anticipated. I miss having endless hours to spend with Noah building puzzles, playing with Legos and creating forts. I realize now how lucky I've been. Mom and Dad enabled me to stay home with Noah until he started school. I won't ever be able to repay them for their generosity.

Standing, I look at the painting still sitting on my easel from a few days ago. Smiling as I remember how much Dax loved it, I find some paper and wrap it up.

"Momma! Uncle Lucas put in the movie, hurry!" Noah skids to a stop in the doorway before bolting back down the hall. Laughing, I quickly finish wrapping the canvas, leaving it on my bed before trailing after Noah into the living room.

Lucas and Noah are sprawled on the couch, so I settle into the beanbag chair Lucas bought for Noah. It was an early birthday present, both of our birthdays less than a month away. Noah was born a week after I turned sixteen. It's hard to believe that was almost five years ago.

The beanbag chair makes a farting noise as I shift to get comfortable, both Noah and Lucas laughing at me. "Oh hush you two."

Ruffling Noah's hair, I turn to the sound of the door opening.

"What are we watching?" Andie asks as she sticks her head into the living room, grinning as Lucas holds up the case for the movie Noah selected. "Noah, I brought someone who I know you are going to be excited to see."

Dax steps around Andie, grinning as Noah screams and jumps off the couch. "Mister Dax! I want you to sit beside me. Uncle Lucas, can he have your spot?"

We all laugh as Lucas slides off the couch, onto the floor next to me. "Darn, I've been replaced."

Settling in, Lucas pushes play, and we turn our attention to *The Lorax*. Noah is talking Dax's ear off as the opening credits rolls. Since meeting him that first day, Noah has idolized Dax. He is always coming up with ideas of what he wants to do with him next.

Shifting my body so I can see them, my stomach gives a little squeeze at the look on Dax's face as he listens to Noah describe all of the places to hide at my parents' house. He is intently listening to every word Noah is saying, not a hint of irritation or boredom. In fact, he looks enthralled. The doting look is enough to make my heart beat a little faster.

Hearing Noah talk fills me with pride. He is so articulate for a boy of his age. Mom says he gets that from me.

"Noah, if you tell him all of your hiding places, how do you expect to have anywhere to hide when he comes over?" Noah's eyes widen as he looks at Dax, who is wearing the biggest smile I've ever seen on his face.

"Don't worry, buddy, I'm sure I will forget." Dax winks at me as the movie starts, distracting Noah, who starts talking his ear off again.

Andie brings out the popcorn, shutting off the lights and we all settle in to watch the movie.

"Ava." A hand shakes me awake and I blink rapidly, dazed. My neck aches, cracking as I tilt my head side to side.

"Hmmm?" Rubbing the palms of my hands over my eyes, I finally focus on the face in front of me. Dax holds Noah in his arms and I realize we are alone. "Where are Andie and Lucas?"

He smirks and tilts his head towards the bedrooms. "They decided to turn in early. You passed out about thirty minutes into the movie and Noah fell asleep shortly after."

He adjusts Noah in his arms and holds his now free hand out to help me up. "Thanks. I can take him." Reaching forward, I giggle as Dax rolls his eyes. "Did you just roll your eyes at me like a sixteen-year-old girl?"

"I sure did. I will carry him." He leads the way to my room, gently tucking Noah into his bed. "Goodnight, Ava."

"Goodnight." Turning to my bed, I see the wrapped canvas and spin back around. "Wait, I have something for you. Here, open it later."

Handing him the canvas, I hold the door as he backs out of it looking confused, smiling as he silently turns to leave. I wait for the click of the front door before I crawl into bed.

The sound of my bedroom door opening wakes me. Sitting up thinking it is Noah, I quickly scramble to pull the covers up over my tank top when I see Dax smirking at me. His smiles are becoming more frequent and the way they change his face makes my pulse race. "Good morning, Sunshine. Thank you for the canvas, I hung it up in our living room." He leans against the doorframe, looking at me in amusement. "Andie and I made pancakes. Get up. We have a busy day ahead of us."

"Huh?" My voice cracks and I resist the urge to throw myself down onto my bed. This is the third time Dax has woken me up, that has to be some sort of weird record.

"Last night, while you were sleeping, we all decided to drive into Jasper today. Do some exploring. Now rise and shine." He shuts the door, the sound of laughter fading as I hear his footsteps move away.

Groaning, I quickly get dressed and throw my hair into a messy bun. Waking Noah up, I have him dressed and ready to go within fifteen minutes.

"Momma, do you think we will see a bear?" He drags me out of the bathroom towards the kitchen, laughing when my stomach gurgles at the delectable scent of breakfast.

"I'm sorry, sweetie, the bears are hibernating right now." Andie hands me a cup of coffee as soon as I step into the kitchen. "Thank you, you read my mind."

"Dax, what does hibernating mean?" Noah sits down at the table, digging into the pancakes Lucas has already cut up for him.

"That's when animals find a nice warm place to sleep until winter is over," Dax answers Noah as he sits next to him. I adore how he doesn't talk to Noah as if he is stupid. He answers all of his questions in a normal tone of voice like he would any person.

"That's a long time to sleep." Noah's eyes are wide as he thinks about the bears.

We finish eating and start bundling into our winter gear. The boys go down to start Andie's SUV so it's warm.

"I never thought I would see the day my brother doted on a child like that. Shows how much he has changed." Andie slips her hat on, waiting for me inside the doorway as I finish wrapping my scarf. "I'm just glad he's not running with Ivan's crowd anymore. Shit got scary for like five years. He would disappear for sometimes weeks at a time."

We silently head downstairs, and I tell myself not to pry, but my curiosity gets the better of me. "Who is Ivan?"

Andie freezes. Right in the middle of the stairs, only speaking when I almost run into her. "Oh, Ava. I probably shouldn't have said anything. He's no one you should worry or think about. Forget I mentioned him."

Yeah, that's unlikely.

Dax

"NOAH, DON'T RUN too far ahead." Ava laughs as Noah plows through the snow. We've been hiking around for about an hour, Noah zig-zagging through the trees and making trails. The sun is blinding reflecting off the snow, so we opted for a path sheltered by spruce trees. It may be cooler, but at least we can see.

"For such a little guy, he sure can push through that snow like it's nothing. I have to admit, I admire the kid's tenacity." I grin as Noah face plants in the snow and jumps up completely unfazed, shaking my head in disbelief.

"I swear he's like the *Energizer Bunny*." Ava watches Noah adoringly, pure love in her eyes. I wonder what it's like to have someone look at me that way.

Noah stops in the middle of the trail and flops onto his back, moving his arms and legs to make a snow angel. "Noah, why don't we build a snowman?"

"Yeah!" Noah jumps up and I'm amazed that his snow angel is not only intact, but also perfectly formed. He starts rolling snow to form a ball and I join in to help him.

"Why don't we make the big one, Uncle Lucas and Miss Andie can make the medium one, and your momma can make the head?" Working with him, we roll out a massive snowball. As we stand back to admire our handiwork, I see Ava standing there holding the snowman's head, watching us with a soft smile on her face. When her eyes meet mine, something flashes across her face before a grin replaces it. She tried to hide it from me, but I'm so attuned to quick observation that I saw the look.

Attraction. I must be mistaking affection for attraction, I hope I am.

"Wow! This is going to be the best snowman!" Andie says as she and Lucas set their snowball on top of ours and Ava finishes it off with the head.

"Noah, stand next to him, and I will take a picture." Ava shoves her gloves into the pocket of her coat and gets her phone ready. Noah grabs my hand and pulls me over to him. We pose for a couple of pictures until Ava is happy with one.

"We should probably turn around and head back. It's almost lunch time and the kid is going to be starving soon," Lucas suggests as he checks his phone.

"We thought we could stop for hot chocolate in town and have lunch there." Andie wraps an arm around Lucas and smiles at Ava.

"Noah, let's turn around. It's lunch time." Ava waits for Noah to go barreling past her before joining Lucas and Andie in the walk back. Lagging behind, I watch the four of them.

Who knew I could have so much fun doing something so normal. Two years ago, I never would have been caught dead hiking in the middle of winter and making a snowman with a kid. I was too damn busy working for Ivan, collecting the debts owed to him and going to parties at his house.

I spent five years with the Vipers. Surrounded by drugs, taking part in beating people for money they owed or underground gambling rings. It never dawned on me that the transition to normalcy could feel so good or be so easy.

It's only easy because they don't know the real you. Not even Andie knows the true extent of how deep I was in and the real reason I finally got out. Thankfully, I owed nothing to Ivan aside from the small job that completed all obligations to him. He couldn't prevent me from leaving and despite the fact he is not a good guy, he stands by his word.

Even when they leave.

Especially when he wants them back.

"You coming, slow poke?" Blinking, I see Ava is walking backward watching me.

"Yeah." Jogging to catch up, I try to ignore the look of concern on her face. I don't deserve that concern.

"Are you okay?" She turns back around and walks beside me, a couple of feet behind Lucas and Andie. Those two are so wrapped up in each other that they are completely oblivious to anything around them, so I watch Noah as Ava waits expectantly.

"I'm fine. Just thinking." Nudging her as she rolls her eyes, I grin and turn the question on her. "What about you Sunshine? Are you okay?"

"Oh, you know. I'm fine. Just thinking." She bends down and scoops some snow into her hands, balling it up. She throws it at Lucas and hits him square in the back of the head. Squealing as he spins around, she runs down the path towards Noah.

It's better to keep her out. I need these people more than they need me. I've done terrible things and it's better off for them not to know.

Looking at Andie and how happy she is since she opened up, I fight off the self-doubt that seems to creep up on me more often than not. She is happier since telling Lucas about our past; maybe that would be the same for me.

Kicking snow in frustration, I remind myself that I don't deserve to be that happy, I need to earn that right.

We finally reach the car and load up, Noah passing out almost immediately.

"Well, I guess we will just head home." Ava laughs as she brushes some hair off his forehead.

"Sounds good. I'm wiped." Andie yawns and looks back at me. "We haven't done anything like that for a long time, have we, Dax?"

"No, Nugget, we haven't."

"Even after Mom left Dad, you became too cool with your badass friends." Andie winks at me to show she is teasing. I don't like where this conversation is going.

"I wasn't too cool, I was too high. Or getting into too much trouble. But thanks." Three sets of eyes stare at me, and I realize what I've just said. "Crap, I'm sorry Andie. I'm just stuck in my head right now, and that wasn't fair."

"It's okay. I'm sorry too." Andie reaches behind her and squeezes my hand.

Turning to look out the window, I avoid the gaze I feel on me. That is more about my history than I intended for Ava to know and I don't want to see the disappointment in her eyes.

The rest of the car ride is silent.

Well, that was a mood killer.

"Dax . . ." Ava's voice is a whisper next to me. "You know it is okay to open up to your friends. Didn't you say the same thing to Andie not too long ago?"

Sighing, I tilt my head down to look at her. Her eyes are clear of judgment. "That's a little different, Ava. That wasn't Andie's fault. She had nothing to be ashamed of. I have everything to be ashamed of."

"We all have things in the past we aren't proud of. Things we feel shame over. Things no one knows. At some point, wouldn't it be nice to know there is one person who knows everything and is still there for you? Whether it's a friend or a lover, it doesn't matter." She looks over to Lucas and Andie, who are talking quietly in the front seat. "If you ever need a friend, I'm here for you. No judgment. Maybe I will tell you my shameful secret."

She turns away from me to rouse Noah and I see we are turning into the driveway for Parkland. "I doubt you have any secret that could be considered shameful."

Sadness fills her eyes as she shakes her head. "You have no idea."

Exiting the vehicle, I ignore everyone as I head inside. Being a part of this group is getting in my head, cracking through my careful facade. It's too much.

CHAPTER 4

Ava

"SOMEONE NEEDS TO distract me before I kick this poor woman in the face." Andie grips the seat of the massage chair she is sitting in, her knuckles white as she avoids the look of the pedicurist warily eyeing her.

"Did you know Dax is a math genius?" Three sets of eyes stare at me and I wish I could take back the words, but that's the first thing that popped into my head.

Dax and I have been in class together for a few weeks now and he seems to be constantly on my mind. Now he's even invaded girls night. I've been fighting this, but my tendency to crush on "bad boys" is the bane of my existence and against my rules. Why can't I fall for a nice, quiet guy? Someone like Jaden. Not that Jaden isn't attractive, he just doesn't have that hard edge that makes me weak. That tough exterior that's so satisfying when you finally crack your way in.

"Oh yeah. I don't know what it is about math and chemistry, but he excels in both of them. He's modest about it, though. I'm impressed he told you." Andie watches as her toenails are painted a blinding florescent green. Her grip loosens on the armrests, and she relaxes into her seat.

"He didn't. We got all of our assignments from the past couple of weeks, and I saw his grades before he tucked them away." I still feel guilty for peeking, but my curiosity about him got the best of me. "Our first class he made it sound like math wasn't his strength."

"That boy has so many things he doesn't like to talk about, why do you think I enjoy torturing him so much?" Kensi leans forward smirking. "He's the strong silent type, and I love trying to drag words out of him."

"He just finds you annoying. I can't get him to shut up." Andie grimaces, her eyes twinkling.

"Sibling relationships are different. He will be a tough nut to crack, and I feel sorry for the woman who falls for him." Kensi leans back in her chair as Andie nods in agreement.

Turning my eyes to my feet, I try to ignore the way those words settle in my gut. Dax may be taking up my thoughts, but we can only be friends anyways, so why does her statement feel like a punch in the gut?

"He may be tough to get through to, but I'm betting whoever accomplishes it will find themselves a fiercely loyal man who would do anything to protect them and make them happy." Nella's words are so soft, I glance at her quickly. She is looking at me and it sinks in that she is talking to only me. Am I that obvious?

"He's not my type." *He's exactly my type.*

"Dax is everyone's type." Kensi leans forward again. By the grin on Andie's face, I realize that they both caught the private exchange between Nella and me. "Everyone knows girls go weak for motorcycle driving, sexy as sin, bad boys."

"I went through that phase and ended up pregnant and alone. I'm over it." Forcing a smile to soften my words, I silently plead with Andie not to take offense.

"Yeah, I can see where that would take away the appeal." She winks at me, and I know they all see through my denial.

"Even if I'm not over it, I won't allow myself to go there.

Besides, he has too many secrets. I don't do secrets." *Liar.*

We shuffle to the dryers and stick our toes under the heat lamps. Andie sits next to me and leans in. "I know what it's like to feel the need to hide something. Dax has done things he isn't proud of. I know all about rules, but I think I recall a certain someone telling me to leap once. Maybe she should take her own advice."

"Andie . . . I just . . . I can't break that rule. If it were just me, maybe I could, but it's not."

She sighs and nods. "I get it. You want a guy like Jaden."

"Are you reading my mind? I was just thinking about him earlier." Laughing, I am always amazed at how well this group of women knows me in such a short amount of time. I'm so lucky.

"But you're not into Jaden. We all know that like we all know Carter has it bad for . . ." Kensi elbows Andie to shut her up. "Oops, right."

"You're right, I'm not. Honestly, thinking about guys is the last thing I need or want to be doing. I'm happy with my friendships and life how it is." It is safe keeping things as they are.

"You know what they say. It finds you when you're not looking for it." Kensi leans around to wink at me. She always has guys on her mind.

Since Noah was born, there has been one interest and it was short lived. I wasn't in a position to share myself, and as much as he tried, he wasn't ready to take on Noah and me. This crush on Dax, it will pass too. I'm not looking for anything and he is such a good friend, I can't jeopardize that.

So I've decided. The crush is fleeting. Friendship is more important. Besides, it's probably a one-way thing, which makes it so much easier. "It will pass. I have my entire life ahead of me."

"Of course. Who wants to show interest in a guy who has bonded with your child, calls you Sunshine and takes an active interest in your life?" Kensi's words are sharp, but that's just her. "If you were Andie, I would be daring you to throw your stupid rules in the trash where they belong and make a move."

"We all have dating rules, Kensi. Mine was no assholes, Ava doesn't want bad boys, and you know you have a thing with anyone in a position of power. Nella, do you have one?"

"I won't date jocks." Nella's voice is quiet, and we all share a look as she checks her phone.

"See, I am pretty sure we all have rules, and we can't always just throw them away." Andie leans into me and rests her head on my shoulder. "So I hear someone's birthday is coming up in February."

Thankful for the change in subject, I jump on it. "Yeah, the third. Noah's is the tenth. We're exactly a week apart."

"What are we doing to celebrate?" Nella asks as we stand to slip on our shoes.

"I'm not sure yet. I need to ask my parents." We leave the salon and walk back to the apartment complex. "Thanks for the girls day. I needed it to clear my head. Tomorrow is the first visit with Joe in months, and I'm a little apprehensive how it will go. I don't know what to do with this new Joe."

"It will be fine. If you need anyone, we're here. You can text all three of us, and we will get you through it."

Andie and I leave Nella and Kensi at their apartment and walk up to the top floor.

She hugs me tightly and even though it's brief, I feel like somehow she shared some of her immense strength with me. Parting ways, I head to my room, a new canvas waiting for me.

Checking the clock, I finally decide to pay and take Noah to change. Joe thought swimming would be a fun activity, so I drove the four hours to Edmonton to meet him. He's twenty minutes late.

"C'mon, Noah. Let's get ready to swim." Taking his hand, I

pay and lead him to the change rooms. Why am I not surprised that Joe flaked out?

"Ava!" Turning, we see Joe jogging towards us. Noah hugs onto my waist, looking at his dad in surprise. "Hi, Buddy! How are you?"

"Hi, Daddy." Nudging Noah, he goes and gives Joe an awkward hug. Joe smiles down at him and instead of the usual look of frustration, his face is simply happy.

"Why don't you change with Daddy and I will meet you at the pool." Ruffling his hair, I watch him run into the men's locker room apprehensively before turning to Joe.

"Sorry I was late. My mom called, and she kept me on the phone in the parking lot for over thirty minutes. She wanted me to invite you and Noah for dinner."

"Seriously?" Joe's parents decided they wanted nothing to do with us, they didn't believe Noah was Joe's until the paternity test, and afterward they let their pride get in the way of any sort of relationship.

"Yeah, Dad had a heart attack two months ago. It's been an eye-opening experience."

"I'm sorry to hear that, but I need to think about dinner. We need to ease into this. We're not a normal family, and I don't want to overwhelm Noah. Now let's go get ready and swim."

"Okay, that makes sense." Taking a deep breath, I push my way into the ladies change room. Agreeable Joe is confusing me. I need to keep my guard up because this is wreaking havoc on my emotions. It's as though someone flipped an attitude switch and I'm waiting for it to be flipped back.

I meet them by the kid's pool and sit on the edge, watching as Joe engages Noah in creative games and actively interacts with him. He had invited me to swim with them, but it's his time with Noah.

Joe completely ignores some girls blatantly trying to gain his attention. He is still very attractive, and I'm not surprised that he has drawn attention. His light brown hair is closely cropped to his head, and his dark blue eyes are filled with laughter as he chases Noah around. He is lean, well-toned and naturally tan. I loathe that I still find him good looking, but thankfully, aside from appreciation for his physical appearance, I feel nothing.

The girls giggle and splash around, looking at him. Subtle ladies . . . very subtle.

He continues to ignore them, and I have to admit, I'm impressed. Smiling as he tosses Noah in the air, he glances over at me and winks. Shaking my head, I try to ignore the fact that my lips twitch in response. He always was charming, even over the past five years I can remember moments where I thought he would be different, that charming person making rare appearances only to slip away just as quickly. My smile fades as I recall all those times I had hope and was let down.

He frowns and leans over to talk to Noah. They both swim over, smiling widely. They quickly lunge towards me and pull me into the water.

"That's it!" Diving under the water, I grab Noah's feet dunking him gently before pulling him up with me as I surface. We splash and wrestle together, Noah's laughter making my heart sing.

"Momma, can we go down the slide?"

"Of course you can, but after, it's time to go home." Noah races off dragging Joe behind him. I'm happy to see that he has warmed up to Joe. It usually goes like this, at first, he is shy, but by the end, he is happy to be spending time with his dad.

Thirty minutes later Joe is putting our things in my trunk and buckling Noah into the car. Shutting the door, he comes to my side of the car and leans against it. "Thank you for today. I know you could have said no. I have no right to ask for more, but you always try to accommodate. I don't deserve that."

"What's going on Joe? Four and a half months ago, I couldn't even get you to come see him in the hospital. Three months ago, you blew us off for a date and just a week and a half ago you called me selfish. Then later that same day you have a complete attitude change. So please, tell me what led to this shift." The onslaught of emotions from watching him actively engage with Noah, trying to include me and the respectful way he has addressed me all day has been a lot to take. My guard is up, and I can't handle not knowing the catch.

"Let's not talk about that now. Can I take you to dinner? I think this would be easier to discuss when we're not freezing our asses off." He opens my car door for me, and I slide into my seat.

"I don't think . . ."

"Please, Ava." He pleads with me.

Sighing, I give in. How does he always manage to get his way? "Fine. I will let you know when I am free." He thanks me and shuts the door. Leaning my head against the headrest, I start my car and berate myself for constantly giving in to him. Curiosity kills the cat, and I have a feeling I'm going to be crushed.

Dax

TOSSING LUCAS A beer as he comes inside, I follow him into the living room where Carter and Jaden are already seated. "Sorry I'm late. I wanted to see how it went today with the visit."

"What visit?" Carter grabs a fistful of chips and tosses me one of the movies he brought.

"Ava took Noah to have a visit with his dad. They rarely happen and usually end up with Ava wanting to shoot Joe and bury him in our backyard." Lucas pulls forward the chair I bought Andie for Christmas and settles in as I push play.

"Sounds tough." Jaden empathizes. No one pushes Lucas to see how it went, they all focus on the Marvel marathon we have decided to tackle this evening.

"She's tough. It took me a long time to realize that, but she really is." He changes the subject to football, Carter's favorite subject. It's his offseason, but the guy lives football. They quit talking as the movie starts, completely enthralled in the Marvel universe.

It takes me a while, but soon the story captures my interest. I haven't watched any of these movies and apparently in this crowd that is unacceptable.

As the movie ends and the credits start rolling, the door to my apartment opens. Andie comes in with Nella, Kensi, and Ava. "Rumor has it you're watching Marvel movies. Please tell me Thor is on this list." Kensi squeezes in between Carter and Jaden with a wink. They grin at her. It is hard not to find her funny. She is so abrasive, but in all the best ways. "Where is Dean?"

"He's on his way. He was just going to stay home, but I told him that wasn't an option." Carter answers, his eyes wandering towards Nella who is on the opposite side of the room from him.

Chuckling, I shake my head at him. "Dude." Catching his attention, I mouth *not gonna happen.* He gives me the finger and stands to put in the next movie.

Looking around the room, I feel content with the group of people I've chosen to surround myself with. No one has hidden agendas, no one is overdosing on whatever drug they took, no one owes anyone else money. It's all so . . . normal.

Ava comes and sits next to me on the floor, leaning against the bottom of the couch. Looking at her, I examine her face closely for any sign of tension. "How did it go today?"

"Surprisingly well. Joe kept Noah engaged the whole time. He focused entirely on his son and not on anything, or should I say anyone else." Her eyes stay on the TV. She is relaxed, but something is up.

"Good. And?"

"What do you mean 'and'?" She tries to shrug off my question, but her fingers fiddle with the hem of her pants.

"There is more to your day than that. You have more tells than a beginner poker player."

"I called Joe out on his change in attitude. He wants to discuss it over dinner. I'm just leery of what he hopes to accomplish. I suspect there is a woman behind it and he wants to start including her in Noah's life." Ava looks at me, eyes filled with concern. "I'm not ready for that. I mean I know it sounds unreasonable. Noah interacts with everyone here, but it's different when it's a relationship and not a friendship. That changes the dynamics. Then I wonder if I say no, does that open me up to criticism if I choose to enter a relationship." Ignoring the way the thought of her being with some tool makes me feel, I try to stay focused on what she's saying.

"This is all so complicated. I never really thought about when we start introducing people to Noah on those terms before. It's a little overwhelming."

"Sunshine, you will figure it out. It takes time. Besides, you know how you said I could always talk to you? Well, that's a two-way street." She nods and her face clears as we both turn to watch the movie.

To my surprise, she inches a little closer and leans on me, looking up at me. "Thank you Dax." Gulping as I see the look in her eyes, I smile and nod at her before returning my attention to the movie. *Fuck. I know that look.* There was no mistaking it this time. I'm no longer friend-zoned.

Andie catches my eye and starts making unsubtle motions, grinning ear to ear. Shaking my head, I give her a pointed look as Ava moves away. She pouts and leans in the whisper something to Lucas. Great. I need to fix this and fast. Ava is way too good for me. I'm scum pretending to be something else. Despite what Ava said, no secret of hers could even compare to the way I've acted. I have a criminal record for fuck's sake.

Something will change that look. Something always does.

Lucas glances over at me, looking like he wants to say something.

"Sorry I'm late." Dean opens the door, a couple of pizzas in hand. Thankful for the interruption, I jump up and give him a hand. Spreading the pizzas out on the coffee table, I grab a chair from the kitchen and go to sit next to Jaden.

Taking a huge bite of pepperoni pizza, I stare down Andie, who is glaring at me. She finally breaks eye contact, and I turn my attention back to the movie, grateful when I see Dean sit next to Ava. She glances at me before turning her attention to the movie, laughing as Dean makes a comment about Thor's hammer.

I didn't miss the hurt look in her eyes.

Ava isn't in class on Tuesday when I arrive, so I set her latte on her desk. Settling in, I glance up and see some guy crowding Ava just outside the classroom. She looks extremely uncomfortable, and I'm up on my feet. Watching carefully as she tries to move past him, I growl when I see him move into her, blocking her exit.

Shoving my seat back, I'm out of the classroom and towering over him. "Let her go before I make you." The words are low, barely containing my anger.

Rather than just walking away, the guy laughs and turns around. He chokes on a breath when he sees how livid I am, my body tense and ready to remove him. He glances back at Ava and I let out a low growl in warning. He scurries away like a scared mouse, but I'm just staring at Ava to make sure she is okay. Her face is a little pale, but her smile lights up her face as she hugs me. My arms wrap around her involuntarily, the primal feeling of pride at how small she feels against me makes me step away quickly. Gently pushing her into the classroom, I follow her to our seats and sit down wordlessly.

My phone vibrates distracting me from needing to deal with what just happened and the physical effect it had on me.

Peyton?

Swiping the screen, I open her text message.

> Dax . . . I need your help. I want out. I don't want to live like this anymore. Please come and get me.

Staring at the screen, I barely hear Ava thank me for the coffee. Realizing I haven't said a word to her, I finally greet her as I always do. "Good morning, Sunshine."

"Are you okay? You look a little dazed." Her face is filled with concern, her eyes looking at the phone still in my hand. She seems to have forgotten what happened in the hall, her concern for me taking precedence.

"Oh, yeah. I just got a text from a friend. I need to pick her up after class today." Ava's face flashes with surprise, and it dawns on me. Peyton will help make that look go away, I can easily make Ava misinterpret my relationship with Peyton, and we could continue being friends. No harm, no foul.

Rather than the relief I expect to feel at this realization, I am disappointed.

Crap.

I tried to deny it. I tried to believe I could just be friends with her, but I've been sucked in. Looking over to where she is flipping through her textbook, I finally open my eyes and see her without the denial glasses I was feebly clinging on to.

Ava is gorgeous. Her dark brown hair, blue eyes, and creamy complexion is everything most people find attractive. Slender, but curvy. She doesn't hit the gym as fanatically as Andie, but she is fit from chasing after Noah.

Attractive girls are a dime a dozen.

More than physically, though, she is smart, artistic, empathetic and observant. She cares about her friends and family. She is strong, witty and makes me laugh. She is everything I would identify in my ideal partner.

I, on the other hand, am less than ideal. Could I ever expect to be enough? Could I ever redeem my past enough to feel that she could be proud to have me on her arm?

Considering how I just responded to that guy hitting on her, part of me doubts my ability to ignore the attraction that's been sneaking up on me.

Realizing I still haven't responded to Peyton, I type out a response. Avoiding the inner turmoil is easy. I've grown accustomed to ignoring things I shouldn't.

> **Dax:** Of course. I will come get you after class. You can have my room, and I will sleep on the couch while we figure everything out.

> **Peyton:** I knew I could count on you. Fuck sleeping on the couch. We've shared a bed before, nothing has changed. And if you've gone all proper on me, I will crash on the couch.

"Well, that should be interesting. I think I better find a cheap futon and make room somewhere."

"Pardon?" Ava looks over at me and smiles, my lips tug in response. How she does it, I don't know, but she never fails to make me smile for real.

"Nothing, I was just talking to myself." She looks so disappointed that I want to punch myself. Even if the side of me that is altruistic wins out over the selfish side of me, I still want to be friends with her. And she did say I could talk so her, so . . ."Sorry, old habits die hard. I need to find a cheap futon somewhere. My friend, Peyton, from my old life of mischief and mayhem, needs a place to stay while she gets her life together. I'm sure it's against housing rules, but I told her she could always count on me."

"My parents have a futon in the basement. I'm sure you could have it. I can ask if you want." Professor Williams walks into the classroom, whiteboard marker in hand and starts jotting down equations.

"I would appreciate that." She nods and quickly types out a text, flashing me her phone to show she inquired.

We've managed to ignore what happened in the hall completely. I want to ask her what's going on in her head, but I don't. The less I know, the better.

It's dark by the time I arrive at Peyton's apartment complex. This area is shady, and I'm glad she won't be living here anymore. Peyton's job within the gang was a blackjack dealer; she loved doing it, so I'm curious to see why she wants out.

Bounding up the stairs, I pound on her door. "Peyton, it's Dax."

The door swings open, but instead of Peyton, Ivan greets me. "How's my favorite drop out?"

"Ivan." Nodding at him, I push past him into the studio style apartment and see Peyton has two small suitcases sitting on the floor. She is seated quietly on the sofa, tears streaking down her pale face. "What's going on here?"

"I just came to remind you both what you're giving up. Playtime is over; it's time to come back. You can even replace Tom as my second in command." His voice makes my whole body tense. Despite his pleasant demeanor, I know the true person that lies underneath.

"I think I speak very clearly for both of us, we're done. We're not coming back. I've made that clear for months, and I will help Peyton. We're not lifers, Ivan. I believe you even said that to me when I first joined." Turning my back on him, I walk over to Peyton and pull her into my arms. "It's okay, Pey. C'mon." She sniffles and follows behind me as I gather her suitcases. She looks so small despite her tall frame, shoulders folded in. That's what Ivan does to people; he makes them feel incapable of surviving.

"You have it all figured out. That's fine. Just remember when you're talking to all your new friends where you came from. Will they still look at you the same if they knew it all? You think you can make up for five years of gang life and have normal relationships. Either you lie or the way they look at you changes." Ivan loses his composure. I've never seen him like this, but his words eat away at me. This is his specialty, shoving your worst fears into your face.

"I guess I can only hope to prove them wrong if that's the case." Resting my hand on Peyton's back, I guide her out of the door.

"You will never be good enough for them, your friends, or potential employers. Once they know the truth, you won't be good enough." His words follow me out of the apartment. One last taunt to haunt me when I'm trying to sleep tonight.

Turning away without responding, I slam the door behind me. Silently, I guide Peyton to Andie's SUV. Holding her door open, I lean in and kiss her on top of her head. "I missed you, Pey."

"I missed you too, D." Closing the door, I walk around the vehicle and get in the driver's seat. "You look good. Don't listen to him, anyone worth anything to you will see past your history. I believe that."

"What changed for you? Last time we talked, you had no interest in leaving." Changing the subject, I grin when I see her roll her eyes. She's like Ava in that sense; she's somehow managed to read me better than most.

"Tom was pressuring me to work in the new club they opened. A strip club. I have to admit, I went and worked there for a few weeks, but I couldn't handle it. Those hands grabbing at me, it brought back too many painful memories. The girls started offering me drugs to cope and last night when I finished a dance, I took something. I can't even remember what, but when I woke up, I had no idea where I was. It scared me, D. I texted you right away." She starts crying again, looking at me with shame in her eyes. "I broke my promise to you. I can never get that back."

Slamming on my brakes, I turn my hazard lights on uncaring that I'm in the middle of the street. Turning towards her, my face is stern as I speak. "You listen to me. You didn't break your promise. I'm here aren't I? You asked me for help when you needed it. That was your promise to me. Now stop crying, it makes me want to resort to violence."

She nods and I start driving back to Parkland. I could kill Tom for putting that pressure on her. We all know her history; she was only supposed to deal blackjack.

"How do you like being a student? Living a normal life?" She pulls the visor down and starts fixing her makeup.

"I like it. Having something to do every day makes being normal easier. Ivan's right, I have secrets, and I am scared they will look at me differently. I've let little things out, but they don't know everything. I'm just trying to do what I'm supposed to."

"Don't listen to Ivan. He's just pissed off because the newest crop of recruitments suck. Dax, you were never meant to be there. Sure, you were good at what you did; you're good at whatever you decide to do. It will work itself out. Me, on the other hand, I was raised in that community. I'm a high school dropout who knows how to deal blackjack and apparently be a stripper. My brother is in the Vipers, and I've been part of that circle since I was nine years old. Nine years of my life spent surrounded by those people. You're going to be okay. I believe that, because if you're okay, you can help me be okay." She reaches over and punches me on the shoulder.

"Let's make a deal. You be my reality check, and I will be yours. Tough love and all that shit." Handing her my phone, I gesture to it, "Text Andie and tell her we're on our way. Her boyfriend's parents dropped off a futon for you this evening. She can't wait to see you again."

Peyton grins at me and nods, typing quickly. "I can't believe it's been almost two years since I've seen her. Now enough sappy shit." She leans forward and turns on the radio, cranking it to earsplitting volumes. Laughing, I join her in singing along to the lyrics of *Earned It by The Weeknd*. We continue to sing along to the radio the entire drive.

This is always our way. Straight and to the point.

Signaling to turn towards Parkland, I grin at Peyton's expression. Turning the music down, I look at her. "If you're going to start fresh, why not do it by the mountains?"

"Wow. I can't wait to see them in the daylight. I've never been to the mountains before." She stares at the apartment complexes, most of them dark. "These are the dorms? I wondered how you were fitting a futon into those miniature rooms from the movies."

"Yeah, since most of the students reside on campus they built apartment complexes. I can't remember how many buildings there are. I'm not a good tour guide." Shrugging, I hop out of the car and grab her suitcases.

"Dax, I won't ever be able to repay you for this." She holds the door open for me and I stare down at her with a glare.

"Don't even think about it. You're family."

Taking a deep breath, I lead her to our apartment. Tomorrow everything will change, the scale is about to tip, and I'm the deciding factor. I'm just not sure if I'm ready for it.

CHAPTER 5

Ava

"AVA! ARE YOU ready? Andie invited us over at ten, it's now five minutes til." Lucas knocks on the door of the bathroom where I'm getting ready. Like I need to be reminded what time breakfast is at?

"Almost." I don't know why I'm putting in the effort to look nice, it's just breakfast. Dax has seen me at my worst before. The difference is, this time I'm meeting someone from his past. A woman. I hate to admit it, but I feel jealous that she knows part of him I don't. The rational part of me says I have no right to feel jealous.

Yesterday he came to my rescue. That guy was not listening to any of my cues, physical or verbal. Dax came storming in like a furious bodyguard. I've never seen him look so terrifying or so attractive. I'm sure I got a glimpse into what he used to be like.

My mind focuses back to the woman I'm about to meet. He called her a friend, and I wonder if they were ever anything more.

Applying one final coat of mascara, I open the door. Lucas stands on the other side waiting impatiently, his foot is even tapping. "Wow! Are we having breakfast with royalty? What's with getting all made up?" He pauses as I shuffle my feet and watches me carefully. I can practically see the lightbulb go off in his head. "Holy shit! You have a thing for Dax and now he has a house guest . . . who is a girl."

Glaring at him as he laughs at me, I brush past him. "Shut up."

"What happened to not dating bad boys anymore? Although compared to Dax, Joe is like a pussy cat." He opens the door for me, crossing the hall. Teasing me loudly. I hope no one hears this.

"Lucas, seriously. We're not dating, he is my friend. I just felt like dressing up a little." Ignoring his knowing look, I open the door and shove him inside. Taking a deep breath, I prepare myself to meet a part of Dax's past, a person who may provide insight into the man who berates himself almost daily because he doesn't think he's good enough. He's completely unaware that he does it; it's so ingrained into his being.

Shit. Haven't I done the same thing? Categorized him as a bad boy and therefore not dateable simply because of the energy he gives off and the fact he has a tough past, rather than recognizing that aside from all of that he has demonstrated on multiple occasions how big of a heart he has, just how generous he is.

I'm a shitty person.

Following Lucas into the kitchen, we both freeze by the sight that greets us. Dax and Andie are laughing as a tall, like model tall, young woman gestures animatedly. Her jet-black hair with vibrant purple tips is cropped in a sexy pixie cut that teases her jaw. Even in oversized sweats and a racerback tank top, she could walk the runway.

Self-consciously, I straighten my body to my full five-feet-nine inches. She's at least five inches taller than I am. The same height as Dax.

"Hey, guys! This is Peyton. Peyton this is my boyfriend, Lucas and his sister, Ava. Ava is one of my best friends. She's the one that painted the sunset you were admiring in our living room." Andie introduces us as she walks over and kisses Lucas.

"That was you? I am envious of your talent. I have no skills like that." Peyton smiles at me, making me smile in return.

"Thank you." Moving to sit next to Dax at the table, I watch Peyton move comfortably around their kitchen. She seems so confident in herself, and I wonder if I exude that kind of confidence. I feel like I think about every action I make before I make it, I wonder if people think about things like that or if it's just me.

We all help ourselves to the food in the center of the table, idly chatting about how good everything looks. Silence takes over the room as we eat and I can feel the words bubbling to the surface.

Taking another bite, I try to hold back my nervous chatter. It's futile, but a girl can try. I manage to hold it in less than two minutes, and I'm counting every second.

"Peyton, if you want to try painting, I have some extra canvases and old paint brushes. I could teach you some fun techniques that I have found to be therapeutic. Not that I'm saying you need that, I'm just saying, for me, it helps me think." Shoving more food into my mouth, I stare at my plate as Lucas tries unsuccessfully to hold in his laughter. I see Andie elbow him from underneath my lashes. Well, I've now insinuated Peyton needs therapy. I'm such an idiot.

Dax leans over and nudges me, waiting for me to look at him. Sighing, I turn my head and meet his hazel gaze. His eyes are filled with humor, and he is smiling at me. "That's very sweet Sunshine." Staring at him as he looks over at Peyton, I slowly follow and see her looking between us.

A slow smile spreads on her face. My gut tells me she just picked up on my crush. Girls are intuitive about that stuff, and I'm ready to crawl under the table and curl into a ball. "I would like that. I am looking into getting my GED since I dropped out of high school, but other than that I have a lot of time." Peyton seems to be genuinely interested, and I admit, the idea having someone to paint with will be fun.

We finish eating and migrate into the living room. Peyton sits on the floor even though there is room on the couch; she seems to shy away from being too close to people. "So how did you and Dax meet?" Lucas asks. I love my brother some days.

"Well, we met five years ago through my older brother. We had the same circle of friends and just clicked. One night some guys were giving me a hard time, and Dax took care of it for me. Ever since then he's taken me under his wing and treated me like a sister." Lucas accepts her response, but it feels vague. It's interesting when you hang out with someone who spends so much time trying not to give too much away you start to pick up on the nuance in others.

"How many brothers do you have?" Curious, I try to learn more about her. Part of me is genuinely curious, even more of me still hopes to learn more about Dax.

"I have three brothers and a half-sister. We're not really close; there is a big age difference between all of us." Peyton scrunches her face in discomfort. She is as uncomfortable talking about herself as Dax is. Fascinating.

"Family isn't always biological. Sometimes the people you choose to surround yourself with becomes your family." Dax smiles and leans back, resting his arm over the back of my chair. Is this an unconscious movement? His arm brushes against my neck, I hold my body very still to resist shivering at the warmth of his arm.

Dax has a tendency to observe everything around him, his words and actions seem thought through and hold a lot of weight. Has he noticed my crush? Some of the things he has said and done seems to have hidden meanings, but I'm overanalyzing things. I have a tendency to do that. The realization that I am unfairly categorizing him based on my previous experience has been eye opening. Have I been acting differently, giving my inner turmoil away?

I wish I could shut my brain off, just be natural, and open

myself to any possibilities. My mind just doesn't work like that, not anymore.

The ringing of my phone startles me out of my thoughts, glancing down I sigh and answer. "Hi, Joe." The chatter around the table silences. Great, an audience.

"I wanted to know when you are free to have that dinner." Lucas narrows his eyes and the realization that everyone can hear the entire conversation puts a stone in my stomach.

"I'm at school until tomorrow afternoon, but I could do tomorrow night. Otherwise it has to wait until Saturday." Keeping my tone friendly, I'm hoping this will be the beginning of a cooperative co-parenting team. I'm not getting my hopes up.

"Saturday works better for me. Why don't I pick you up, you drove for the visit." My arm kind of droops and I stare at my phone for a moment before lifting it back to my ear. That was actually thoughtful.

"Oh. Umm, thank you."

"How does six o'clock sound?"

"Perfect, I will see you then." I'm still in shock at the difference in our conversations as we say goodbye, and I hang up.

"Did you just set up a fucking date with Joe?" Lucas gapes at me incredulously, not bothering to hide the disapproval in his tone.

"It's not a date. We're discussing our plan for Noah and what the hell brought this change about." I'm defensive, and I know it doesn't add credibility to the words I'm saying. Lucas opens his mouth in what I'm sure will be an impressive lecture, holding my hand up to stop him I push my chair back. "I appreciate the breakfast, guys, but I'm feeling a little sick. Please excuse me."

Exiting the apartment, I feel instant relief. The last thing I need is to deal with this in front of everyone. I'm perfectly capable of managing Joe on my own. Groaning as I shut the door to my bedroom, I regret leaving so abruptly. It was rude,

and I could have just shut Lucas down instead.

Flinging myself onto my bed, I close my eyes and ponder all the changes in my life. It seems like everything is happening at once and even though it's all been good so far, I find it overwhelming trying to compartmentalize my life.

Life is messy, and I know better than try to do this, but as I lay there, I find it soothing to section off the areas I need to deal with knowing that at some point they will collide.

Dax

THE DOOR SHUTS quietly behind Ava, everyone staring at the empty space by the door.

"I feel like I'm missing something." Peyton breaks the silence.

"Joe is my nephew Noah's father. I use the term father very loosely. He broke her heart and has been a jackass to her ever since." Lucas grinds out. If it wasn't for the hold Andie has on his arm, I'm sure he would be out that door and giving Ava a piece of his mind. "Recent change of heart aside, I don't trust him."

Looking down at the empty chair beside me, I ponder the idea that this could be a date. She seemed defensive. Jealousy surges through me that he might have a second chance when I haven't even earned the right for a first one.

"I think we're going to go for a walk. Peyton, I will see you later." Andie drags Lucas out the door and I'm sitting silently with Peyton.

"What a welcome. I'm sorry about that." Gathering the dishes, I load them in the sink and start filling it with soapy water.

"Shit happens. Anyways, they're fun. I like them; Ava seems funny. She doesn't like silence does she? Like at all."

"Picked up on that did you? It's one of my favorite things about her." Smiling, I hand Peyton a plate and shake my head. "If you stay silent long enough, you learn some funny and random things. It's cute."

"Interesting. When are you going to admit you both like each other and make a move? If this is a date, you're running out of time." Staring at the plate I'm washing, I scrub at a spot vigorously. Fuck, I forgot how Peyton always seems to be riding the same train of thought I am. Peyton rests her hand on my arm, stopping me. "That plate is clean. D, you have done well for yourself here. These people, they are part of the family you choose for yourself. Ava is different, though, I know you see the way she looks at you, but what you're missing is the way you look at her in return. Don't miss your chance."

"I don't think so." With the dishes finished, I have nothing to do with my hands, and I desperately need to end this conversation. Her words have the potential to give me false hope.

"Shut up and listen. Reality check. You are not the sum of your past choices. Who you are now is a result of you choosing a different path, regardless of whether you were not so gently guided to that choice. You are a better person than most. The way you look at her, that doesn't happen often. You know I wouldn't make this shit up."

"I need to think about it. I don't know if my kind of baggage is something she can handle." Crossing my arms, I ponder how to ease Ava into my past. Do I even want to subject her to the horror stories?

"Only one way to find out. Besides, the woman had a kid while in high school. I'm pretty sure she is stronger than you're giving her credit for." Peyton refills her cup of coffee and leans against the counter. "I'm going to go sign up to complete my GED. By the way, there is a dick-shaped water stain on your ceiling and that is not something I can unsee." Winking at me, she saunters out of the room.

Ava is in class when I arrive with our coffees. "Hi Sunshine, how are you?" Handing her the caramel macchiato I bought her as I sit in my seat, the uneasiness I'm trying to block out makes me feel nauseated. I've never been this nervous for anything in my life, including sitting in court waiting for a sentence. Glancing around the classroom, I'm relieved that it's still fairly empty.

Ava looks up from where she is doodling, fresh paint covering her hands, her smile lights up her face. I've never had someone look at me quite like she has before. The attraction, yes, but with Ava there is no hidden agenda. She doesn't want to use me as a stepping ladder to get anywhere, in fact, she would probably get further without me. "Thank you. I think it's my turn to start bringing coffee in the morning. You've been keeping me caffeinated for a month now, we should switch."

"Nope." Grinning as she gives me her best stern look. Peyton stripped away at my careful control, giving me false hope. I'm at risk of falling, and if I fall, I'm at risk for getting fucked. Even if she can accept my history, it was ingrained into us from the start—if you let people in, they can be used against you.

That's not your life anymore. I repeat it in my head over and over, trying to make myself believe this isn't just a lucid long ass dream. Inhaling deeply, I devour her with my eyes, searching for a way to keep my last foot in the friend zone. She's already opened the door; I just need to make the move, but I don't know if I should.

Her eyes have flecks of green that I never noticed before, every emotion she feels on display. Ava has the perfect heart shaped face, her skin looks incredibly soft. More importantly, she doesn't look at me the way other people do. She doesn't look at me with eyes full of assumptions, or automatically flinch when I scowl.

Ava clears her throat, staring at me questioningly.

"You never told me how your day is going." She smiles as I shift uncomfortably in my seat. I feel fucking vulnerable, and I can't stand it.

"It's going okay." She pauses, her hand doodling on her page. I don't think she is even aware she is doing it. "How about you?" She grins, waiting for my typical vague answer.

"It's been weird having Peyton back in my life. In my gang

days, she was there every day, but it feels weird having her here. Not bad weird, just different weird. I never thought my old world and this new one would collide." Shifting uncomfortably again, I glance up at her to see her reaction to my words. She is staring at me in surprise. "That doesn't make any sense, does it?"

She closes her eyes for a second and takes a deep breath. I'm holding mine; waiting for the emotions I dread will be in her eyes . . . fear, judgment, disgust, disappointment, superiority. When she opens her eyes, it's not fear I see, it's something different . . . something I can't quite pinpoint. "No, it makes perfect sense. When you experience any kind of life change, there are things or people you think you will leave behind forever because they just don't seem like they will fit in your new reality.

"I can relate in a way. When I got pregnant, I tried to maintain my friendships exactly how they were, but my life was not the same. Some of my friends adapted with me, and we became closer than ever, although most of my friends distanced themselves because they didn't like my new reality. I couldn't begrudge them of that choice, we were fifteen. Just like having Peyton here is almost like a test, it's a test to see how you can both adapt to her being a part of your life in a different capacity."

Professor Williams chooses this moment to step into the classroom, lecture at the ready. Looking around, I'm surprised to see the desks are full. Somehow, Ava manages to shut off the part of my brain that is always on guard. Terrifying as that is, it's exhausting to be tense and ready for whatever all the time. When I first sat down I was nervous and on edge, now I'm surprisingly relaxed, in awe that she seems to understand what I meant so well.

"I want you to break into teams for today's assignment. It's going to be a lengthy project working through the statistical analysis problem on page one fifty of your text, remember you each need to complete your own, but with partner work it shouldn't be as daunting." For once, I'm glad for partner work and turn to Ava as Williams starts writing formulas on the white board.

"Well partner, I guess I have permission to cheat off you now." Winking at her, I flip to the correct page. "So, what you said . . . who knew you were so wise? That's exactly how it feels. I keep wondering if she is going to fit in."

"Wise? You must be kidding me. And she will do fine fitting in. I've never met a group of people who are so accepting of each other." She has a point. Our group is incredibly diverse, something I never thought possible. Although I'm starting to open my eyes to the fact that I have locked myself in a small box, and it's time to get out of that box. It's time to stop limiting myself based on misguided beliefs. Things that have been ingrained into me by Ivan and the gang culture meant to keep you captive to that life.

Ignoring her remark about being wise, I quickly work through the first question in our assignment. "True. That's not what I was expecting when I started making what Andie calls 'healthy friends.' I spent years being told no one outside of the Vipers would accept us." My mouth feels like it's full of cotton balls as I try to open up a bit.

Ava's face is soft as she smiles at me. "Well, whoever told you that is an asshat and completely wrong." Her words contradict the look on her face. She is soft and open, her words strong and . . . Protective? The cotton balls slowly disappear as we buckle down into the problem. Ava has a knack for statistics, which makes it easier to continue carrying a conversation with her.

Too quickly, Williams draws our attention back to him. "Okay, next week I want this assignment done. There will be no more classroom time for it, so please coordinate yourselves." Many students groan as they realize they will have to collaborate outside of class, and Williams scowls at them. "Despite what you may think, in many jobs, regardless the field of work you choose, require you to work in groups or with a partner. Suck it up and get it done, you're adults now, and that requires you to do things you don't want to do."

Laughing, I turn to Ava. "Okay, he may be dull when he's

lecturing, but I like him." She nods, the look of happiness gone from her face and replaced with nerves. "What's wrong?"

"I need to leave for dinner with Joe. Something came up Saturday, so he is picking me up here in like ten minutes. I'm worried about what he needs to tell me that he couldn't over the phone." She fidgets with the strap of her bag, looking up at me with her brow creased in worry. "The thing is, Joe had a bit of a right to be angry with me in the beginning. I'm ashamed to say I deserved some of it. Don't get me wrong, he should have gotten over it much sooner, but this change in attitude makes me worry. I want to believe it's genuine, but I also don't want to get my hopes up."

"Okay, first of all, what could you possibly have done to deserve the way he treated you? Secondly, you know you have a ton of support from all of us and, more importantly, your parents, if he tries to pull any shit."

"No one knows the whole story of when I got pregnant. It's not something I'm proud of and it's not something I thought I would ever share. You see . . ." Her phone starts ringing startling both of us, and she answers it with a shaky hand.

"Hi, Joe." I can't hear what he's saying, but from the expression on her face, I'm guessing he is here. "Okay, I will be right out." She hangs up the phone and looks at me, eyes wide and hands shaking. "Well, I guess my story of shame needs to wait until another day. I couldn't stand it if this was karma coming to make me pay for past mistakes."

"Don't be ridiculous. You are an amazing mother, and karma isn't going to make you pay for something you did when you were fifteen. If that's the way it works, I'm fucked." Resting my hand on the small of her back, I nudge her towards the door. "I will walk you out and when it's over and done with you know where to find me if you need to talk it out."

Instead of dropping my hand like I should, I leave it there. It's a dick move, I still don't even know if I plan on acting on my attraction, but I'm staking my claim. She may not realize it, but he will.

CHAPTER 6

Ava

MY BACK TINGLES where Dax's hand rests, the heat from his palm spreading warmth throughout my whole body. It doesn't even cross my mind that his hand almost feels possessive until I feel his fingers flex on my back as Joe's eyes narrow at the sight of us walking towards him, eyes drawn to where Dax's hand rests.

My heart drops in disappointment when Dax's hand falls away from my back as we stop in front of Joe. "Joe, this is my friend Dax. Dax, this is Noah's dad."

The guys eye each other up, Dax's jaw clenched and tension radiating off him. Joe is the first to look away, and I can honestly say I don't blame him. Dax stares him down, his gaze intense and fierce. The fact that I used to think Joe was so hot because he was a bad boy is laughable.

Joe looks at me without either of them saying anything. "Are you ready to go?"

"Yeah." Turning to Dax, my words fail. He is still looking at Joe, who is now waiting in the car, jealousy clear across his face. Shaking my head, I clear to that wishful thought, he's probably just worried. Nudging him with my elbow, I recapture his attention. "We need to work on that math project. So I will call you later, okay?"

He nods, moving to stand between the car and me. "If you need a ride home from wherever, you feel free to call me." My pulse starts pounding as he rests his hand on my arm, gently squeezing. The hopeless romantic that still resides inside whispers that he is holding me back, that he doesn't want me to go. The logical part of my brain tells me I'm reading too much into it, like I have a tendency to do.

He opens the car door for me, sending a warning glance towards Joe.

Joe silently pulls away, I watch Dax walk away without a backward glance and wish I were walking with him. "Where are we going?"

Sighing, Joe glances at me before focusing back on the road. "I thought we would go into Jasper, since they have some cute cafes we can find a quiet booth in."

"Sounds good." Grabbing my phone, I quickly text Lucas to let him know where we will be. I forgot to mention the change in plans with Joe, although I'm relieved that it's now chatting over coffee and not dinner.

"So your boyfriend . . ." Joe starts, and I can tell I'm not going to like where he is going with that sentence.

"I'm going to stop you right there. He is not my boyfriend, but even if he was that topic is off limits. We are sorting out our own bullshit today." He gapes at me; I've never talked to him like this before. Staring him down, I wait for him to acknowledge my limit before releasing him from my gaze. "Good. So why don't we get this started. You have spent the better part of six years actively avoiding being involved in anything to do with Noah, and quite honestly making my life more difficult. So, what do you want, Joe? I've spent enough time with you to know that you only act so compliant when you want something."

Crossing my arms, I stand my ground. It's taken me a long time and a lot of soul searching to learn how not to let him bring me to my knees. The guilt I felt over that night made me feel at his mercy; while that guilt is still there, I know that there, are more important things to consider.

"Wow. Okay, I'm not used to this side of you." He looks at me in surprise before winking. "It's pretty hot. Reminds me of when we first met, do you remember?"

Sighing, I stay firm. "Joe, what are you doing?"

"Lightening the mood." Fighting the twitch in my lips, I hate that he still knows how to push some of my buttons. He smirks when he sees the twitch and laughs. "Fine. I know I have been an asshole, can we just say I grew up?"

"No."

"It's taken me a long time to get over being angry with you. It may not have seemed like it, but I loved you, Ava. I never thought you would lie to me like you did. As time went on, I got over it, but it took a while and by then it seemed too late to try to have a different kind of relationship with you.

"Then Dad had a heart attack and as a family we've been doing some reflecting. Dad was disappointed that he almost risked a relationship with his only grandchild simply out of pride. I think we all realized what we have been sacrificing." Joe pulls into a quaint little coffee shop.

Stunned by the information overload, I silently follow him into the building. He gestures to two cozy armchairs by a lit fireplace. Taking a seat, I watch him place our order. I shouldn't let him buy me coffee. This isn't a date, and his flirtatious comments are inappropriate. I know how much a significant life event can cause someone to change. My pregnancy caused my whole family to change. Part of me, the small part that had held onto hope Joe would've come around, is angry that my pregnancy didn't do this for Joe.

Joe hands me my latte as he sits across from me. "So why did it take so long for you to act on this epiphany? Your actions didn't change or the way you spoke to me." I'm still skeptical that there isn't more to this story. Once the haze had lifted from my eyes, I had seen how manipulative Joe had been when we were dating, I had also become more like that, and I don't ever want to be that girl again.

A girl I didn't even like at the end.

"It's simple. Pride. Besides, I knew you would be skeptical. No one would blame you. So I'm here to say that I will do anything in my power to demonstrate I want to be a good father." He leans back in his chair and watches me try to sift through his words for any holes.

"Okay then." I want to believe him; I want to think that Noah could have the best of both his parents, so I choose to give him the benefit of the doubt.

Joe smiles as he relaxes a bit into his chair. "Okay then."

"Well, if that's it why don't we head back?" Joe stops me as I move to stand, shaking his head as he swallows nervously.

"That's not it. I have a . . . proposition for you."

Narrowing my eyes, the sinking feeling in my gut is back. I should have known. "What kind of proposition." Each word is enunciated, my voice sharp with worry. I suspect I know where this is going, and it could ruin what little progress we have made.

"I want us to try again. I want us to try to make our family whole." Joe reaches out and takes my hand. Shocked, I let him. This is not what I was expecting. "We had a good thing, we could have it again."

Removing my hand from his grasp, I sputter at his description of our relationship. "A good thing? Joe, do you not remember what our relationship was? Fooling around and fighting. We both became so manipulative with the other that we lost sight of who we were. I don't want to become that girl again, I hated her." Shaking my head, I can't seem to get ahold of my body. These are the words I had wanted to hear when I told him I was pregnant. When I was too young to recognize how unhealthy we were. "Besides, I heard a woman's voice over the phone the other day. Are you seriously trying to start something with me when you have someone else?"

"Ava, that was my therapist. Besides, the first time we dated we were kids. It's different now." His words are soft, his eyes hopeful. My mind stutters over his confession of seeing a therapist. Part of my heart clenches, I can't stand letting someone down. Even someone who has hurt me as much as he has.

"No. I'm sorry. I don't feel that way about you. Please take me back to Lucas's." He nods silently, disappointment clear on his face. Standing, he opens the door to the cafe once again surprising me with the thoughtfulness behind his actions. He never did this when we were dating. Pausing, I try to think of words that convey how much I appreciate his effort. Something holds me back, though, so I thank him for holding the door and leave the rest alone.

The drive back to campus is quiet, the radio playing softly in the background. For once, I don't feel the need to fill it, I just want to get to my paints and forget this mess. As Joe shifts the car into park, he turns to me. "Can we set up a schedule for when I can see Noah?"

"Of course. Goodbye, Joe." Getting out of the vehicle, I shut it and walk away.

The sound of the window sliding down stops me. "I am not giving up on this idea. I will prove to you I have changed, that we have changed, enough to be good together." I don't turn around; I just walk into the building and right into Dax.

Dax

"EASY THERE, SUNSHINE." Holding Ava steady, I laugh softly as she stares at me in a daze. "You all right? I didn't think you hit me that hard."

She shakes her head and smiles at me. "I'm fine. Sorry I ran into you, I'm not normally so clumsy."

"That's nothing compared to Andie." She seems to be steadier, so I let my hands drop slowly from her arms. She looks up at me, her breath catching as we stare at each other.

"Right, she is a sight to behold some days." We hold each other's gazes until the movement of her throat as she swallows catches my eye. All thoughts except my need to taste her flee from my head. Ever since watching her drive away with another man the only thing I could think of was how I couldn't risk losing my chance. I can always work towards being good enough later.

"I don't want to talk about Andie though." My pulse thunders as I move my eyes up her throat, to her lips. Aching to close the gap, I gauge her response.

"You don't?" Meeting her eyes, I shake my head. Her expression is clear of whatever was preoccupying her when we collided. "What do you want to talk about then?" Her words are quiet as she whispers the question we both know she has the answer to. Her eyes dilate in what I hope is anticipation.

"I don't want to talk." Stepping into her, I drown in the way she smells, the way her breathing picks up. Ignoring how my pulse has kicked up, I try to move slowly. Tilting my head down, I brush my lips against hers; they are soft and respond immediately to my touch.

A soft moan erupts from her throat as I gently press into her, and all of my control evaporates. Digging my fingers into her hips, I push her against the wall. My tongue strokes against hers as I deepen the kiss, grinding my body into her willing embrace.

Moaning as she fists her hands in my hair, pulling on the ends, I break free from her kiss and brush my lips softly down her neck. The little throaty noises she is making are sexy as hell, pressing my lips back onto hers I'm overwhelmed by every sensation flooding my nervous system.

Breaking away, I gently glide my fingers along her jawline. Her lips are swollen, her eyes glazed with desire. "Okay then. Have a good night." Stepping away from her, I turn to the door and casually try to adjust myself.

I'm halfway out of the door before she responds. "Seriously?"

Turning around, I almost forget where I was going before she ran into me once again. Her hair is wild and the hand propped on her hip screams attitude. "Yes. I have things to do."

With that, I shut the door behind me and count to ten trying to gather some self-control.

Fuck it. Opening the door, I take the steps two at a time, catching Ava in the second-floor landing. Spinning her around, I pull her into me, crushing my lips to hers. Dragging her with me as my back finds the wall, I hold her close, kissing her with bruising vigor. She is responding with just as much intensity, her throat humming in desire.

Her hands are in my hair again, pulling with just enough force.

The part of my brain that is still functioning tells me I should stop and get her out of the hallway, but the other part wins out as she presses her body more tightly into mine.

"Ahem." Ignoring the throat clearing, I hope whomever it is will move on. They do it again and I growl a little before lifting my head to see who is interrupting us.

Kensi and Andie's smirking faces greet me. Groaning, I drop my head to Ava's shoulder before straightening up.

"Hi, guys." Kensi grins as Ava turns away from me; I avoid looking over at her. My self-control is hanging by a tattered thread, and I'm barely able to prevent myself from grabbing Ava's hand and dragging her up the stairs.

"You know, we have to walk here." Andie winks at Ava, who laughs good-naturedly.

"Well, don't let us stop you." Glaring at both of them, they tauntingly wave as they pass by us.

"Maybe take your activities outside of the hall, you know before clothes start dropping." Kensi quips before turning the corner.

"Go to hell, Kens."

"See you there." Andie laughs as I hear her tell Kensi to hush.

Their footsteps disappear before I finally look at Ava. She is watching me, looking stunning as she searches my eyes. Ava and I have never talked or expressed any interest in being anything other than friends, not in words at least.

I know I should fill in the silence, but instead I wait. She shifts in place and I fight the smirk I can feel itching to pop out.

Her hands fidget with the hem of her shirt, her eyes shifting between mine as I watch her. I can see the words bubbling to the surface.

"You're an amazing kisser. I mean, I never doubted otherwise. It's been a while for me; I guess you could probably tell. What? Why?" She takes a deep, shuddering breath. She shakes her head and smiles to herself, when she looks back up at me her eyes are glittering with humor. "Scratch that and insert something sexy and witty."

"You want me to take you upstairs so you can ravish me? Well, seems a bit sudden, but how can I say no to that?" Winking at her as she glares playfully at me, I start backing up the stairs.

"I asked for that." She shakes her head as she follows me up the stairs. The moment has passed and the rational part of my brain says that we need to slow down.

"So . . . math class." She laughs at me, shaking her head in disbelief. "Why don't you come over and we will finish that assignment?"

"Okay." She looks disappointed as I turn to walk beside her. I know we need to talk about what just happened. It's not fair to leave her in limbo, but I'm still figuring out what exactly is going on. All I know is that when she ran into me, I felt the need to claim her more intensely than I have ever felt before.

Several hours later, we are both hopped up on caffeine and junk food. "Well, I think that had to be one of the longest math projects I've ever been subjected to." Ava leans back on the kitchen chair, stretching her arms above her head. My eyes are automatically drawn to the glimpse of skin that briefly appears before she lower her arms. Her skin is flawless, begging for my touch.

Her eyes widen as she catches me checking her out, my body reacting to the blatant desire she isn't trying to hide. A sexy little smirk lifts the corners of her lips as she crosses her arms accenting her curves. My body feels like it's on fire, my arms aching to hold her.

We both stand, shoving the chairs out of our way. Grabbing her hands, I wind them back into my hair. Our lips mold together passionately, pressing into each other urgently. Gripping her hips, I set her on the kitchen table, groaning when she wraps her legs around my waist.

Burying my face in her neck, I lift her off the table, set her on her feet, and step away. The sounds of disappointment she makes are so sexy, and I'm not about to quit, but I don't want any more interruptions. Sliding my hand into hers, I lead her into my room and lock the door.

Ava steps into me, pulling my head down to hers. Breaking away, I find the hem of her shirt and lift it over her head before lowering her onto my bed. Kneeling down, I explore her body devouring her with my lips.

Pushing away, I remove my shirt and lay on top of her. My cock throbbing as our bodies grind together, her nipples peaked through her bra. Pulling the cup down, I suck a nipple into my mouth, grinning as Ava arches into me.

Moving to the other breast, sucking hard as I unclasp her bra.

Our hands are feverish as the rest of our clothing finds its way to the floor, all thoughts of moving slow a distant afterthought. Every movement feels primal, lost in the needs of our bodies.

Her legs wrap around me as we move together. Ava pulls away, panting for breath. "Condom?"

Nodding, I silently chastise myself for almost losing control. Fumbling in my nightstand, I find one and tear it with my teeth before sheathing myself and slamming into her. "Dax." She gasps my name, her body clenching around my dick as she adjusts to my size. She's so fucking tight.

Thrusting into her wetness, I almost lose my load when her eyes fixate on where we join. Resting on my elbows, I keep my pace while devouring her mouth with mine until we're both gasping for air.

"Harder." Her command takes me by surprise, her voice raspy with passion. Pulling back, I pound into her harder as she moans nonsense in response. Her pussy is wet, and soon she is clenching around me like a vice as her orgasm rips through her.

Before she has a chance to come down from the wave she is riding on, I pull out of her chuckling as she curses at me. Flipping her onto her front, I grab her hips and lift her. Slamming into her, I quickly find my pace again. Ava pushes back into me, soaking wet as she gasps out, "Pull my hair."

Groaning, I fist my hand into her silky locks as I move faster and harder. I fucking love that she isn't afraid to demand what she needs. It's such a damn turn on. She meets me thrust for thrust, and I lose my load as she comes again, collapsing underneath me, her body glistening with sweat.

Drawing back, I plant kisses down Ava's spine before standing and leaving the room to clean myself up.

It's not until I'm standing outside my door that I'm struck with guilt. What the hell have I done? I've just had sex with Ava without even taking her on a date first. I'm supposed to be changing myself, not fucking doing the same old shit. Ava deserves more. She is not some for now kind of girl.

"Shit." Muttering to myself, I slowly walk into the room and sit on the bed. Ava turns towards me, her smile fading as she sees my face. She jumps out of bed and quickly starts pulling on her clothes, her body shaking.

"Well, I don't need to ask what's going through your head." Her voice is thick with held back tears and the anger I feel at myself intensifies.

"You don't know shit. So before you go storming out of here like a typical girl, sit your ass down." Clenching my jaw shut, I want to punch myself for not thinking my words through.

Ava turns and glares at me, tears gone, body shaking with anger. She walks over and shoves me on the shoulder. "Don't. Don't you dare speak to me that way." She goes to leave, but I catch her arm and pull her onto my lap. Wrapping my arms around her, I hold her to me.

"You're right. I'm sorry, but I needed you to not storm out of here. I have no regrets that we had sex. My regret lies in that I didn't even take you out for a date first. I'm not proud of my past choices, the thought of letting you down is more than I can handle and I've already failed in doing this right. There is an order that things should be done and I've fucked it up." Loosening my hold as she relaxes, I take a few deep breaths to ease the tension in my body.

"Don't be ridiculous. If I'm not mistaken, it takes two people to have sex. This was consensual and damn amazing until about two minutes ago." Her voice softens her words, her hand back in my hair. Closing my eyes as she teases the strands, I hum in pleasure. "Not every relationship has to take the same path."

Grasping her hand, I remove it from my hair. "I can't think straight when you do that."

Ava rests her palm against my chest and pushes me down, curling into my side. "Stop thinking. Sometimes getting stuck in our heads is the worst thing, trust me, I know. Now, can we get back to what was a pretty damn good evening?"

"I'm going to take you out. This isn't just scratching an itch. I hope you know that." I feel Ava smile against my chest.

"Okay."

Finally, the remaining tension leaves my body leaving me exhausted. With Ava in my arms, playing with my hair, I fall asleep.

CHAPTER 7

Ava

SLAMMING MY CAR door, I slip inside my parent's house quietly. Dad has a meeting early in the morning, and the last thing I want is to wake him up.

"Ava?" Jumping at my mom's voice, I look at the stairway to see her standing there in her nightgown.

"I'm sorry, Mom, I didn't mean to wake you. Go back to sleep." Whispering, I step up onto the step next to her and kiss her cheek.

"I'm a mother; I will always wait for you to get home." Nudging her up the stairs, I follow her up and peek in on Noah. I feel bad for slipping out on Dax while he was sleeping, but I wanted to be here to drive Noah to school in the morning. "You know, I'm going to want information on this boy tomorrow morning after you drop Noah off."

"How did you know?"

"Mom radar." She kisses my forehead and shuts the door to her bedroom.

Collapsing onto my bed, I think about what happened with Dax this evening. This could be a huge mistake, but that's a risk I'm willing to take. My crush for Dax is more than I can ignore and after tonight, well every part of me is on board with seeing where this goes. My hesitation dissipated as soon as he stepped into me, taking charge of the most amazing kiss I've ever experienced. Body aching in the best way, I quickly fall asleep with thoughts of Dax flitting through my head.

My alarm goes off way too soon and the urge to hit snooze is overwhelming. My phone buzzes next to me and I grin when I see a text from Dax light up the screen.

> **Dax:** My bed was cold and sad when I woke up this morning. I feel a little used ;)

> **Me:** I had to get home to take Noah to school, and I didn't want to wake you.

> **Dax:** Can't complain, it's not a bad way to be used. I just had hoped for an encore this morning.

> **Me:** What happened to taking me on a proper date?

> **Dax:** Oh, that's happening. And sooner rather than later.

My face hurts from the grin it's sporting as I ponder how to respond. The door to my room flying open startles me, a small blur runs in and tackles me.

"Momma! Can we play in the snow?" He is bouncing on my bed, a buzzing whir of energy.

"Noah, you have school today." Kissing all over his face, my heart swells as he giggles and tries to kiss me right back.

"Grandma said school is cancelled because of all of the snow. See?" He opens the curtains in my room to a complete white out.

"Sounds like fun, but let's have breakfast with Grandma first and then we can play in the snow." Noah races out of the room, whooping in excitement. I don't know where he gets his love of snow from, certainly not from me.

Glancing back to my abandoned response to Dax, I type the first thing that comes to mind.

Me: I hope so.

Leaving my phone on my desk, I follow my nose to the kitchen where I see fresh waffles on the kitchen table.

"Good morning. Fill your plate and then start spilling the beans on your life." Mom winks at me as she hands me a plate and goes back to the waffle iron.

"I just saw you a few days ago. What makes you think I have a lot to tell you? I mean maybe it's nothing, just a look or a smile." Taking my first bite, I lift my eyes to the ceiling in ecstasy. "These are delicious."

"I know. Now talk, because I could tell last night that there are things I want to know." She sits across from me, handing Noah cut up waffles, before turning her entire focus on me.

Watching Noah devour his food, I try to figure out where to start. "I don't even know where to begin. I guess with Joe."

Filling her in, I speak low, so Noah doesn't pick up on the subject matter. Mom makes sympathetic noises when she hears about his father, but her demeanor changes as soon as I mention Joe wanting to try being together. "Obviously I said no. I mean, I know I was something of a terror in the time we were together. Not to mention the years that have followed. Even if I thought it was a good idea, which I don't, I don't think we could get past that."

"I'm glad he wants to be more active and I'm glad that Noah's other grandparents are coming around, but I'm even more happy you aren't considering pursuing a relationship with him." She passes me a bowl of strawberries and looks at me expectantly. "Now get to the dirt."

"There is this guy in my circle of friends, Andie's brother. You met him around Christmas. Well, he kissed me yesterday. He wants to take me out, and I'm kind of really excited." Giving the mom appropriate version, I smile when I think about last night.

"Kind of really excited? That's an oxymoron." She winks at me as I stick my tongue out at her. "Well, I look forward to seeing him again and grilling him. You know, I need to make sure he's good enough for you and my grandson."

"Mom . . ."

"I have the perfect time! This Sunday I want to celebrate your birthday since it's on Monday. Invite your friends. Then I can meet him again in a more casual way." She looks like the Cheshire cat, she is so proud of herself.

"That's actually not a bad idea. I will send Andie a text and she can rally everyone. Now, I better go play in the snow with my son before he decides he can't wait any longer."

"Have fun, I will have hot chocolate waiting for you when you get cold. We should watch a girly movie tonight after Noah is in bed. I will paint your nails." Leaning down, I hug her tightly. I am so blessed to have amazing parents.

Collapsing on the couch next to Mom that evening, I sigh in exhaustion. "That boy, he has more energy than ten children. He wanted me to read him three stories and, of course, I can't say no to that face."

"You better learn how. Otherwise, you are going to have your hands full when he is a teenager." Mom wraps me into her arms, squeezing affectionately. "Now, since all of your friends are coming over, we need to decide what you want me to cook."

Pushing play on the movie, I curl into my mom's comforting embrace. "You know my favorites. You decide."

"Ok, I'm going to have fun with it, though. I think we need to make it a theme party, so I'm going to contact your brother, and you can be surprised." She is practically quivering with excitement.

"Should I be worried? I feel worried."

"Don't be silly, it will be great. I will even convince your dad to participate." There will be no talking her out of this and to be honest, I'm excited to see what she comes up with. Mom is incredibly creative and always throws the best parties.

Steam wafts from my bathroom as I enter my room, smiling when I see the dress Mom has laid out on my bed.

Alice in Wonderland, the *Tim Burton* version. She knows me so well.

Excitement hits me as I try the baby blue dress on, twirling in front of the mirror. Quickly taking it off so I don't mess it up, I set about getting myself ready.

Sitting at my vanity table, a birthday gift for my eighteenth birthday, I set my hair in rollers before meticulously applying my makeup. Instead of trying to get it exactly like the movie, I take some artistic liberties.

Tilting my head as I complete the smoky eye, I finish with a soft blush. Carefully checking my hair, I quickly unroll it and spray it with copious amounts of hairspray. Running my fingers through the curls, I slide back into the dress and check out the final look.

Barely holding back a squeal as I swish the dress, my excitement diminishes a bit as the doorbell rings. The nerves take over as I realize that Mom and Dad are going to meet Dax as more than just Andie's brother, now he means something to me. They have been incredibly protective of me since Noah and the thought that they may not like him because of the energy he tends to put out sets the butterflies in my stomach into a flurry of activity. I want them to see past the tough exterior like I did almost right from the start.

Taking a deep breath, I exit my room towards the sound of voices. The low rumble of Dax's voice stands out, it's so sexy that my body is at war trying to decide if it's nervous, turned on or excited. I haven't seen him since we slept together, but we've chatted every day. Nervous to see how this evening goes, I try to steady myself before seeing him.

Peering around the corner, I slap my hand over my mouth as

I see my friends all dressed up. They look hilarious and incredible. Dax is the Mad Hatter, hair teased in a way I didn't know possible and face all made up in bright makeup.

Inhaling, I start down the steps, eyes on Dax. The nerves are winning out, how do I greet him? The entire group will know about our make out session by now thanks to Kensi, but we haven't really established more than he wants to take me on a date.

Dax looks up at me, his hazel eyes widening as he slowly looks me up and down, caressing me with his eyes. Freezing in place so I don't fall, I'm captive in his gaze, and I don't ever want to be free. The world falls away as he strides towards me, my breath caught in my lungs.

This man is dangerous.

Dax

MY FEET MOVE before my brain has caught up to my body's response. Ava looks absolutely stunning, and the only thought in my head is the need to be close to her. Forgetting where we are, I take the few remaining steps towards her and rest my forehead on hers.

"Wow." Slowly inhaling, I stare into her eyes as I try to find the words I need to describe exactly how spectacular she looks. "I'm at a loss for words. There is not a single word in the English language that can describe just how beautiful you are."

Her eyes shine, and I can't control myself any longer, I need to taste her again. Leaning down, I capture her lips with my own in a soft kiss before I step away from her reluctantly. That one kiss felt like the first sip of water after being deprived for too long.

We have an audience, which seems to be a trend when I kiss her and the fact that her parents are standing in the room has managed to break through the fog in my head.

Turning around, ready to face probing eyes, I'm shocked to see the entrance has cleared out. Voices come from somewhere else in the house. "They're in the kitchen." Ava's voice is soft as she steps down next to me and looks up, her hands teasing the tips of my hair as she pulls me down, her lips eagerly pressing against mine.

Leaning into her, I press her against the wall and deepen the kiss. Her hands pull my hair harder, her lips devouring mine. Reluctantly, I pull away. Everyone in the kitchen knows what's happening on these stairs.

"Well, I guess that's a way to make an impression on your parents. What do you do to me? I forget where I am with you." Intertwining my fingers with hers, I pull her into my arms reveling in how it feels to hold her.

"I don't know. It's never been like this for me." Her whisper is so soft, I don't think I'm meant to hear her. Tilting her chin up, I brush my lips against hers, unable to resist the temptation.

"That makes two of us. I guess we can figure out how to navigate this together." Everything feels so fast. We went from being friends to having sex in the blink of an eye. Skipping everything in between that should have been done, I feel like I failed her, but I know if I voice that out loud she might yell at me again.

She may be okay with the order things happened, but it will be a regret for me. A slip back into old ways.

"What's with you two and stairs? Come on, you have got to see what Jules has done in here." Andie stands at the bottom of the stairs, smirking at us. Resting my hand on Ava's lower back, we walk into the kitchen together. Both of us unsure and unsteady about what exactly we're doing and how to make our way through these overwhelming emotions.

I can't speak for her, but I feel like I've been submerged all at once sputtering for air as I try to keep my head above water.

"Mom! You . . . I . . . Holy shit." Ava sputters and I finally really look around the room.

The table is set in the midst of lush green vines and foliage. Each table setting is different and made up with toadstools, teacups and napkins shaped into animals. I don't even know how she managed it.

The food smells amazing and is stored in baskets or uniquely shaped pottery dishes all over the table. It's funky and cool.

Ava leaves my side and wraps herself into her mom's embrace. That's when Noah comes in the room, dressed like Tweedle-Dee or Tweedle-Dum. The laugh that escapes me is unavoidable. "Dax!" Noah runs up to me, wrapping his arms around my waist.

"Hey, Buddy!" Crouching down, I straighten one of his suspenders and hug him. "Your costume is awesome!"

"Grandma made it. It's Momma's birthday tomorrow." He continues talking about how he helped Ava's mom decorate and how hard it was to keep the secret. "Can we play hide and seek?"

Laughing at the abrupt subject change, I stand up and look over to where Ava is talking with Lucas. "We better ask your momma if we can play later. I bet if you ask really nice we will all play."

Noah runs over to Ava talking excitedly about everything. Smiling at them, I feel someone looking at me and turn towards the table. Ava's mom is walking towards me, her expression serious.

Trying not to look too intense, an automatic expression for my face when I'm feeling apprehensive, I hold out my hand as she stops in front of me. "Hi Mrs. Jensen, it's nice to see you again. I apologize for earlier."

She ignores my hand and pulls me into a hug. "Call me Jules." She steps back from me, her expression serious and I freeze. "I've never seen Noah quite like that with anyone except his Uncle. It's something special, which means you're someone special."

Without saying anything, she walks away from me, leaving me stunned.

"Okay, let's all dig in while the food is still hot. Rumor has it that afterwards an epic game of hide and seek will commence so you're going to need your strength." Jules winks at Noah as he bounces in his seat.

"Sit beside me." Ava slips her hand inside mine, filling the void I never knew I needed to be filled until her, pulling me towards the head of the table.

Carter, Jaden, and Dean are the only ones who couldn't make it, the rest of our group including Peyton all surround Ava. They are loudly showing their appreciation for the meal Jules prepared.

"Mom, this is incredible!" Lucas's mouth is full and before Jules can scold him, Andie elbows him in the side.

It doesn't take us long to finish eating. "Mrs. Jensen, that was delicious. Thank you so much for having us." Peyton's voice is soft. She sits beside me, and I can tell this whole experience has been overwhelming for her. She's used to crowds of people, but not settings like this. She grew up moving from family member to family member before being removed and placed in a foster home. By then she was disenchanted with the whole "family" situation and ran away to join the Vipers.

"Anytime you all want to come over, you're welcome to. It doesn't matter the day or time, someone is always here." Jules smiles warmly at Peyton. "Now why don't you play that game of hide and seek while I get the cake ready."

Noah jumps out of his chair and is running out of the room before any of us have stood up.

"I'm tired already." Lucas jokes before racing off after his nephew.

"I will count." Nella volunteers, sitting back down at the table and closing her eyes.

Looking at my remaining friends, we all laugh and race out of the room. Dragging Ava with me, we search for the perfect spot. "You're hiding with me."

"I know just the place. Honestly, I never get tired of this game. That's something I love about being a mom, I have an excuse to still enjoy the things I never want to grow out of." Ava leads me to the basement where she pulls open a door that blends so well in with the wall I never would have expected it to be there. "This used to be my fort. I've been saving it for Noah's birthday next week. Until they find Lucas, no one will be able to find us here."

Getting on my hands and knees, I crawl into the room blinking as Ava turns on a lamp. The ceiling is low and covered with brightly colored curtains giving it a tent-like feel. Pillows cover the floor in piles creating cozy areas to sit or lie down. "Well, this is really damn cool."

Feeling the warmth from Ava's body behind me, I turn around. Her lips are on mine, arms wrapped tightly around me before I've even processed her movement. *She makes me forget to be on guard.* That thought flies out of my head as she nudges me into a pile of pillows, straddling me without lifting her mouth from mine.

Breaking away, I pull her down next to me and rub my finger gently over her lips, smirking as she pouts. "I know your birthday is tomorrow, but how is this birthday measuring up to previous ones?"

"Best one yet. Honestly, I love celebrating my birthday. I don't care about gifts, but spending time with family and friends doing something fun always makes me happy. It's also when I do most of my reflecting on what I want to change or accomplish over the next year. I think my twenty-first year will be a hard one to beat." Her hands find mine and I hold them up, looking at our fingers clasped together.

The smile that crosses my face when I see pink, orange, and purple paint staining her hands faintly is inevitable.

"What's so funny?" She pulls her hands away and starts inspecting them closely.

"I love that no matter what you always have paint on your hands. It's one of the first things I noticed about you. The ever changing colors surrounding your finger-nails or staining the tips." Grabbing her hands back into mine, I hold them close. "Tell me something about you I don't know."

"I can't curl my tongue. Lucas used to mock me all the time, teasing me by curling his and then laughing when I wasn't able to." She scrunches her face and laughs softly. "Your turn."

"I can curl my tongue, but I don't want to upset you, so I won't demonstrate." She squeezes my side in just the right spot, causing me to seize into a little ball. "Oh and I'm very ticklish right there, so much so that I accidentally elbowed someone in the face once and broke their nose."

Ava drops her hands from my sides, her eyes wide. "Good to know."

The sound of voices outside the closed door catches our attention, and she puts her fingers to her lips as she crawls and turns off the lamp.

We're both blinded as the door swings open and Lucas peers in triumphantly. "I knew it! Kensi, you owe me twenty bucks, they're not naked."

"Damn!" Kensi's face appears and she glares at me as she slaps a twenty-dollar bill into Lucas's waiting hand. "You let me down."

"Hey! Watch what you say, where is my kid?" Ava's sharp "mom" voice comes out, and they both have the good sense to look ashamed.

"He's upstairs helping your mom put candles on the cake." Andie's voice carries from behind Lucas.

Crawling out of the fort after Ava, we exit to the room and shut the door. Kensi leads the charge back to the kitchen, Ava falling into step beside me at the back. Stopping her outside the kitchen, I kiss her lightly on the lips. "Best game of hide and seek I've ever played."

Smiling, she steps into the kitchen to a chorus of voices singing happy birthday. I move to stand with the group and watch her blow out the candles, her eyes finding mine as the last flame is extinguished.

CHAPTER 8

Ava

LUCAS LEANS BACK, the kitchen chair balanced on two legs, his brows raised as I stumble into the kitchen. "Coffee." My voice is rough from just waking up and I blindly reach for a mug and pour myself some coffee. Breathing in the aroma, I lose myself in the rich flavor as I gulp back the caffeinated goodness. Feeling a little more human, I pour myself a second mug and sit down at the table, ready to savor this cup.

"I'm surprised you're here and not shacking up with Dax." He narrows his eyes at me and despite the teasing tone, I feel the unspoken words.

"You're not planning on going across the hall and kicking some ass are you?"

Lucas drops the chair back onto all four legs with a solid thud. "Nah. Dax is a good guy. I'm just disappointed I heard about you two from Andie and then witnessed it myself at your party. We haven't had much time to chat lately. That's partially my fault." He leans forward, his expression serious. "Have you thought this relationship through?"

"Honestly, not really. It's happened so fast. We need to take several steps back and have some serious conversations. Being a parent and dating doesn't exactly give me the leisure of taking my time in discussing the future, especially since Noah is attached." Sighing, I'm relieved to be voicing some of my concerns. Lucas looks at me empathetically.

"No, not exactly."

"Can I ask you something?" Wringing my hands together, I wait for his nod before continuing. "Andie and Dax are both so closed. I'm not sure how to get him to open up and there are things we both need to share."

"Well, your situation is a little different, but just be direct. If you open up first it will make it easier for him." Lucas stands and refills our cups before dropping into a chair closer to me. His face is serious as he examines me. "How does Noah fit into all of this? That's something you need to figure out as well."

"I know. I'm scared. Noah is part of being with me, and that's long term, I'm not quite sure how to broach that subject either." Lucas just stares at me, and I laugh. "I know, just be direct. This is so hard."

"If you want this to work he needs to be aware what that entails, including your expectations." He reaches over and squeezes my hand.

"Thanks, Lucas. I guess I know all this, it's nice to talk it out, though."

"Anytime." We finish our coffees, Lucas putting the mugs in the dishwasher. Leaning over, he kisses the top of my head. "Love you Ava."

"Love you too."

An hour later, my phone vibrates with the reminder that I need to leave and meet Joe. He decided for Noah's birthday that he wanted to take us to see some new movie that he thinks Noah will like. I tried to convince him to take Noah without me, and I would go shopping with the gift certificates I got for my birthday, but he said no. I had explicitly said that for the first several visits, I needed to be there, and he is holding me to that because now he has a motive for me being there.

Sighing as I look at the cards in my wallet begging to be spent, I call Noah. Everyone wanted to get me art supplies, but since they don't know what I need, they pitched in, and I now have one hundred and fifty dollars burning a hole in my pocket.

Noah is already standing at the door with his shoes on, bouncing in place. "What movie is Daddy taking us to see?"

This is the second visit with his Dad in a month, a record for Joe. He's also taken up FaceTiming with Noah a few times a week, so for the first time in a long time, Noah is actually excited to see his father. I'm happy about this, I'm not happy that since Joe told me he wanted us to try again he has been actively pursuing me.

Flowers on my birthday. A good morning text every day.

He is determined.

"It's a surprise Little Man. Let's go and maybe we can convince Daddy to buy you some popcorn." Opening the door, I follow him to the car and buckle him in. Looking to the sky, I pray that we can just have a good afternoon.

We arrive at the theater early, but Joe is waiting outside the doors with a birthday gift for Noah. "Hi, Daddy!" Noah walks up and hugs him, smiling when Joe ruffles his hair.

"Hey, Kiddo. Happy Birthday!"

"Daddy, my birthday is tomorrow." Noah scrunches his face in confusion.

"You're right, I just don't get to see you tomorrow so you get to open a present early." Noah grins as Joe hands him the gift and we go inside to find a place to sit.

"Ava, why are you over there? Join us." Joe reaches towards me, dropping his hand at the last second.

"Momma, see what Daddy got for me." Unable to deny Noah, I sit down next to him and watch him unwrap his gift. Noah opens the box and gasps as he sees what is inside. Eyes wide, he sticks his hand in the box and pulls out a Nintendo DS. "Thank you, Daddy!"

Noah jumps out of his seat and onto his father's lap. Joe looks at me over his shoulder, "I hope that's an okay gift?"

"It's a great gift." Checking in the box, I smile when I see the two games he bought are decently educational. "We better go get our seats."

Joe nods and takes Noah's hands. "Are you excited, Noah? We're going to a dinosaur movie!" The two of them get popcorn and even though having Joe consistently around isn't easy, seeing the smile on Noah's face as he finally gets to spend time with his dad makes it all worth it.

Together we head into the movie, Noah sitting between us. I only hope that it's not confusing for him once I'm no longer coming on the visits.

Two hours later, we are exiting the theater, Noah talking excitedly about his favorite parts. Joe rests his hand on the small of my back as we walk to the car, dropping it when I flinch. It was an unconscious reaction, but that's where Dax has taken to resting his hand and it doesn't feel right when Joe does it.

Aside from a few awkward moments, the visit has gone well, and I have to admit, Joe has been impressing me with his commitment to showing he is devoted to being a better father. I just wish he would give up on the hope that we can make things work. Five years ago, this change in attitude would have had me melting into a puddle at his feet. I'm not a scared sixteen-year-old anymore, and my heart is definitely not available. It's been giving pieces of itself away for over a month now.

Closing the door to my car, I turn to Joe taking a step back from his nearness. "I think that we should up the time you get with him. Let's do a visit a week for the next month, if they go well, we will add in sleepovers."

"Done. When are you free for the next one? Do you want to set a day? Maybe Fridays?" He leans against the car and smiles crookedly at me.

"Not Fridays. Let's do Sundays. With March around the corner, you can plan more things outdoors and when we do sleepovers Mondays are good for me to pick him up in the morning." Trying to coordinate a second person being so involved in Noah's life is something I know I need to do, but the idea of him not being at my parents' house causes me some anxiety.

"Are you going to sleep over the first time too?" Joe's voice is teasing, but I catch the serious undertone to the question.

"No, I'm not. Joe, I have no issue co-parenting with you, however aside from an amicable, platonic relationship in which we discuss our son, there is nothing else." Disappointment fills his face before his smirk is back.

"I told you, I'm not giving up. Don't make any rash decisions." Before I can stop him, his lips are on my cheek in a brief peck. He steps back and opens my car door. "I will see you next Sunday."

Shutting my car door, I bang my head against the headrest of my seat. That is going to be exhausting. Closing my eyes, I try to figure out the best way to shut this down for good without damaging the progress we've made in regards to Noah. My phone dings with a text; opening my eyes, I fish it out of my purse praying it's not Joe.

Dax: Why do you look so tired?

Perking up, I look around and almost squeal out loud when I see him, Andie and Kensi parked in the spot across from me. Removing my key from the ignition, I open my door.

"What are you guys doing here?" Leaning on my door, I try to slow my heart as Dax walks over to me.

"The girls wanted to do some shopping, and I tagged along because I was hoping to catch you before you left. Why don't I ride back with you, Andie can pick me up from your parent's after they're done spending money they don't have." He stuffs his hands in his pockets and for the first time, I see Dax looking unsettled. He's putting himself out there, something I know is difficult for him.

"That sounds perfect. Noah will fall asleep as soon as we start driving, so the company would be appreciated." Waving at the girls, I slip back into my car and glance at Noah. He's already asleep.

Dax gets in my car and turns down the music, checking on Noah he turns back to me and smiles. "He sure is a cute kid. A year ago, the idea of being around kids was not something I even considered. Now, honestly, I think having to consider my actions and words more carefully is making me better. All of you are making me better."

"I don't think you give yourself enough credit. Like I've told you before, we all have things in our past that we're not proud of." I look at him out of the corner of my eye as I turn onto the highway. We are locked in a car together for two and a half hours. We've jumped into something that neither of us knows what it is, and I don't have the luxury to be flighty in my relationships, especially when Noah is already attached, and he doesn't know what's going on.

"Ava, you may not think the same if you knew." Dax looks out the window, his jaw clenched so tight mine is experiencing sympathy pains.

"You're infuriating! Didn't you give Andie a lecture for basically saying the same thing? What about the fact that you could learn things about me that may change the way you view me? Isn't the whole point of getting to know each other to decide whether whatever this is will work? We've jumped in pretty quickly, so let's skip over the bullshit lovey dovey crap and dig right in." Inhaling, I try to calm the pounding of my heart. This is a two-way street. I have an idea of what kind of shit Dax used to get into, I googled the Vipers and it was eye-opening, but will he be able to accept me for my past mistake?

"You're right; we're not taking a normal route into a relationship. I don't open up easily, I'm not proud of my past, and it's not something I want to share with most people." Dax looks at me, intensity radiating off him. It's overwhelming. "I don't think I'm good enough for you. I don't know if I ever will be, but I can try."

"That's all anyone can ever ask. And isn't it up to me to decide whether you're 'good enough' for me?" Inhaling deeply, I find a side road and pull off. Unbuckling my seat belt, I turn towards Dax. "The night I got pregnant, Joe walked in on me having sex with his best friend. We'd had a fight the day before and said a lot of terrible things to each other and I was trying to get back at him."

Closing my eyes, I'm flooded with shame at how vindictive I was. "I had been holding out on Joe and then gave it up to his best friend, knowing the likelihood we would get caught was high. He stormed out of the room and started drinking. I found him alone later, and we started fighting. Then we started kissing. One thing led to another and well the result is sleeping in the back seat." Turning my head towards him, I let the pain I'm feeling seep out into my words. "I told him not to worry about a condom. I made the choice that got us into this. The thing is, I won't regret it. I cannot regret anything that led to Noah. What I do regret is the person I was when he was conceived. Joe didn't believe that Noah was his because there could have been a chance it wasn't. No one knows this. I'm so ashamed that I would use sex as a weapon like that."

Fidgeting with my parking brake, I stare at my lap. Fingers brush against my jaw as Dax gently tilts my head towards his, his lips meeting mine briefly. "No one expects you to regret Noah, and if they do, they don't deserve to be in your life. Besides, I don't know of any fifteen-year-old that isn't vindictive or manipulative. Your choices have molded who you are and who you are is pretty damn great."

"Remind yourself of that when you're giving yourself a hard time." Gripping the sides of his head, I pull his forehead down to mine. "Your turn."

He nods, forehead scrunching as he leans against the door and watches me shift into gear. I'm assuming it will be easier for him to talk if I have to watch the road instead of him.

"I need to ease into this. You will have to give me time to tell you everything and I'm not going to sugarcoat anything. Some of it will have to wait until we're alone." He reaches down and clasps my hand in his. Dax's grip is firm, but it's manageable.

"I joined a gang, the Vipers, when I was fifteen. At least I think I was fifteen, I spent a lot of time under the influence of drugs until I was seventeen. I was not a nice person, there was a lot of anger, and I let people use it for their own gain." He tries to turn away from me, but I grip his hand tighter and pull it into my lap.

"Don't." He looks at me, his thoughts elsewhere. "Don't shut down."

"It's hard not to fall back on the coping mechanisms I've been taught. It's easy to tell other people not to do things; it's more difficult to tell yourself the same thing." Squeezing my hand, he looks straight out the window, jaw working as he struggles to voice the words he needs to. "If something I tell you causes you to look at me differently, I don't know how I will handle it. I've spent the better part of a year being told no one will accept me so I should just come back to those that do. I've been told it so much, I believe it."

"Have you killed anyone?" I say it jokingly, but we both know I'm serious.

"No." His voice is low, controlled.

My shoulders lose the tension I was holding. I hate myself for allowing that doubt to fill my head. He feels my reaction, and I can sense him closing off a bit. Clutching his hand, I try to take away the damage that question caused. "I know that, even if my brain questioned it, in my heart I had no doubt." As I say the words, I know they're true and he can tell they are too.

Lifting my hand, he kisses the palm before releasing it.

Dax

MY HAND FEELS empty without hers, but I can't be touching her when I tell her what I need to. The words that will ultimately change how she sees me. Checking the back seat, I'm both relieved, and disappointed Noah is still asleep. I have no excuses. "I've never killed anyone before, but I've beaten someone to the point of hospitalization. All for the sake of a small debt they hadn't paid to someone else. I was a tool, a merciless tool."

Silence surrounds us as she drives, her eyes focused on the road ahead. Looking at the clock, I'm shocked to see we've been driving for over two hours. Counting the minutes she doesn't say anything, I feel dread slowly fill my body.

Different outcomes fill my head.

She's terrified.

She's disgusted.

She's realizing she's too good for someone like me.

She accepts it.

The last one is almost the worst because it means I would have allowed Ivan to manipulate me one last time, allowed him to make me believe that someone as wonderful as Ava would never see past my transgressions and accept me wholly.

It's been ten minutes since anyone has said anything. I feel myself locking up, prepared for the worst. She takes the exit towards her parents' house, turning into their driveway way too soon.

As soon as the vehicle is parked, I'm outside trying to breathe when it feels like a fist is crushing my lungs.

Ava's car door shuts quietly, her footsteps crunching on the gravel until she stops in front of me. Closing my eyes, I can't look her in the eyes as she tells me how disgusting I am.

Gentle hands cup my face. "You need to forgive yourself. Someone saw a person who was damaged. Saw someone who needed a role model, a strong figure in his life and took advantage of that. Are you responsible for the decisions of your past? Absolutely. That doesn't mean it's unforgivable."

"You are either the most understanding person I will ever meet, or you are in denial of what I admitted to you." Opening my eyes, I search her face for any trace her words don't match what she is feeling inside.

"I understand you perfectly. I also know you are not that person any more. Do I have any doubt you will do whatever is necessary to protect those you love, no. I only have one question." Her thumbs make soft circles down my neck to my shoulders, easing some of the tension I've been carrying since I told her part of my past. There is so much more to say, but I'm not going to pile it on all at once.

"Anything."

"Is there any part of you, any part in the slightest, that misses it and is tempted to go back?" Ava looks at me steadily, the strong woman she is shining through.

"None at all." It's not even an option, not if I want to finally be someone worthy of her and definitely not if I want to stay out of prison.

Her responding smile is brilliant, relief flooding through me as she steps into my arms.

"Promise?"

"I swear. I'm never going back."

"Okay then." Ava tilts her head up, pulling me down into a fierce kiss.

It's shocking how difficult it was to force those words out, but seeing how accepting she is I want her to know all of me. I don't want her to have any question about who I am and I want the same from her. The want, the need, to know everything about her is growing. This woman has the capacity to become more to me than I ever thought possible.

"I think it's time I finally take you out on a first date."

She chuckles and nods, turning to open the rear car door and lifts Noah from his seat. Leaning down, I take him from her arms. Ava smiles gratefully, her expression soft as she grabs the rest of their things from the car.

Together we walk into her parents' house, and I tuck him into his bed as she goes to let her mom know we're going out.

Watching Noah curl into his pillow, arm wrapping around a stuffed koala bear, the enormity of what I'm getting involved with really clicks. Instead of feeling overwhelmed or scared, I'm shocked to find I feel excited.

This scenario seemed out of reach for me. No one would ever think I was deserving of this, but as Ava slips her hand into mine, I realize that I've found someone who sees past everything else and sees me. For the first time, I feel content.

Grabbing my phone to text Andie that Ava is going to bring me home, I pause as I see a message from Robert. Crap, I forgot it's time for my quarterly meeting with him. One more thing to explain to Ava.

CHAPTER 9

Ava

DAX OPENS THE door for me, my stomach tied in knots as we walk into the intimate restaurant together for our first official date. The low lighting creates soft shadows throughout the small dining area. There are no tables, just intimate booths providing privacy to the diners.

"I know dinner seems kind of cliché, but I thought we should do something normal for our first date . . . Since we skipped over this step." Dax's hand rests on the small of my back, heat spreading through my body to the point I can't even hear what the hostess is saying as she leads us to a quiet corner.

"This is perfect." I'm finally able to speak as we sit down, thighs touching under the tablecloth.

Silently, we look at the menus. My knee starts moving as the silence grows. I can see the twitch of Dax's lips as he feels it. He knows I start babbling when no one talks for a while, and it's worse tonight because I'm nervous. I'm positive he waits for me to burst with embarrassing chatter on purpose.

Ridiculous seeing as we've seen each other naked, yet I know myself, and I know that us being on an actual date makes this officially real. That means the fact that I'm falling in love with

97

him is something I need to address. Not only with him, but also with my family and with Joe.

It seems completely ridiculous to use that word so quickly, but there is not a single thing about him that I don't love.

Dax reaches under the table, engulfing my hand in his and squeezing. The nerves settle, and even though I still want to break the silence, it's simply because I want to talk to him. I want to hear what he is thinking about, I want to learn everything about him.

"I don't even know what your favorite color is." He lays his menu down. I haven't even really seen what's on it as I set mine down as well.

"It's orange. The orange that takes over the trees in the fall." His answer is perfect. I don't know how picking a favorite color can have a right or wrong answer, but his is the right one.

"That's funny, mine is the color of new leaves in the spring. That vibrant green." I see the server making her way towards us, so I quickly scan the menu.

"Hi, I'm Tammy. What can I get started for you this evening?" She eyes Dax appreciatively, blushing when she sees me watching her.

He looks at me to go first. "May I please have an iced tea to drink and I would like the lemon chicken with a Caesar salad and the garlic mashed potatoes."

She jots down my order quickly and turns to Dax. I can't blame her for wanting to look at him, and surprisingly, I'm not jealous at all. I know he notices that she is eyeing him appreciatively, Dax sees everything, but he doesn't pay any attention to it as he looks at her. "That sounds perfect, I will have the same." He hands her our menus, smiling politely before turning to face me. "How old were you when you started painting?"

"I was six. It's something Mom and I did together. She loves arts and crafts, even to this day our house is decorated with homemade decorations every holiday. She is addicted to Pinterest and trying out anything she has time for." It's hard not to feel guilty talking about how wonderful my parents are when I know that Dax and Andie had such a tough upbringing. I've met Char, I think she is wonderful . . . now.

Andie told me not that long ago that when she took Lucas to Calmar to visit her mom she found antidepressants in her bathroom. Remembering the relief she had that her mom had finally gotten herself some help, I couldn't help feel angry that she didn't try harder when her children were younger. Then again, I can't imagine being in their mom's position either.

"Before we realized what kind of person my dad is, we used to do family fishing days. We would find an obscure lake somewhere. Dad would help me fish. Mom and Andie would play cards or build a fort. Thinking back on those days, I wonder how we ended up where we did."

Dax pauses as the server sets our drinks in front of us with the promise our food will be ready shortly. I don't even look at her, the faraway look on Dax's face distracting me. "It makes me wonder what changed, because I don't think Dad was always the person he is now. I used to worry that whatever happened to him would happen to me . . . I still worry about it sometimes."

Folding myself into Dax, I try to think of anything to say to make him realize how different he is from his father. No words seem to be enough, but the feeling that I need to say something overtakes me. "Dax, your dad isn't well. Maybe things were better in the beginning, but that doesn't mean a lot didn't happen that you weren't aware about. There is no doubt in my mind that you will never turn into your father."

He rests his chin on my head. I know he is far away reflecting on whatever he sees of his father in himself. Waiting for him to come back to me, I ignore my phone when it vibrates in my pocket just holding onto him.

Sometimes I still see the look in Andie's eyes as she seizes up, getting lost in her past. Both of them have that same tendency and I can only hope that one day I can bring Dax back the way Lucas can bring Andie back.

Dax releases a heavy breath and pulls away, smiling as my

phone vibrates again. "Kinky. Why didn't I think of bringing toys to dinner?"

Winking at him, I go along with it. "There is a lot you have yet to learn about me, but don't worry I fully intend on teaching you." The periodic vibrating doesn't stop and I'm sure I have at least ten text messages. "I'm sorry, it might be my Mom."

Pulling my phone from my pocket, I groan when I see that while Mom did text me, once, I have nine other messages from Joe. "Wow, he's really pursuing you, isn't he?"

Dax grins without shame as I look up to him peering down at my phone screen. "It's exhausting, but I don't know what to do about it. I've already told him it's not going to happen."

Reading the text from my Mom, I quickly type out where I left Noah's *Nintendo DS*. Shutting my phone off, I slip it into my purse turning back to Dax as the Tammy chick brings us our food.

"I can't say that I blame him. I would regret letting you get away too." Dax's grin is cheeky, and I'm glad to see he doesn't seem to be stuck in his head anymore.

"Yeah well, sometimes second chances are impossible and this is one of those times." I scoop a forkful of mashed potatoes, groaning as I take my first bite. "These are amazing. I would apologize for the garlic breath, but I cannot regret these potatoes. Anyways, even if Joe had stuck around, we would never have lasted. Some relationships are not meant to be. They are too hard and they bring out the worst in people."

Dax moans as he tries his potatoes, distracting me from my train of thought. He is so sexy, and I love that it's just who he is. He isn't posing or trying, he just is. "There, now we both have garlic breath." He breathes out the word breath making me laugh. I've rarely seen him act silly and usually it's with Noah. "You're right, some relationships are toxic. Others bring out the very best in people. They encompass all that is good and possible when you find the right person. Couples like Lucas and Andie."

"Like you do for me." The words slip out of my mouth before I can stop them. I couldn't help it, as he was speaking all

I could think was that Dax brings out all of my favorite things about myself. Looking at him, frozen in place, I wait for him to process that I just called him my soulmate without using that word. Do I even believe in soulmates? I think I do now.

"I was going to say that to you. I've never felt worthy and it didn't bother me until I met you. Don't get me wrong, I wanted to straighten out and fit in with mainstream society, but aside from proving to myself, I could, I didn't look any further. Then you happened. Everything to this point has been moving so fast, but for whatever reason it has felt right." He laughs lightly. "Insert a manly comment here, because I'm pretty sure if the guys were here they'd revoke my man card."

Elbowing him in the side, I grin. "Your secret is safe with me. At least until I have a girl's night and spill the beans that you're a softie." My brain processes the words that I've said the second I quit talking. My breath catching, I hope that Dax realizes I'm teasing. He's opened up so much today; I wouldn't want him to think I would ever betray that. Dax stays silent and my verbal spewing rears its ugly head. "I mean obviously I wouldn't say anything you didn't want me to. I only meant that I would say that you have a soft side. Unless of course you didn't want me to say anything at all. I don't need to say anything. They will ask, but I can control myself. Not that I'm demonstrating that very well right now. I need to stop talking now."

Clamping my lips shut, I focus on cutting the perfectly cooked chicken before me, avoiding any eye contact with Dax. It's not until I finally have to gasp for air that I realize he is shaking with laughter. "Relax. I have spent enough time watching Andie and Kensi to understand how girls' night works. I trust you, Ava. If I didn't, I wouldn't be here."

"I guess I know that. Sometimes I just worry that some of the things I say will be misinterpreted. It's been known to happen before, and not everyone deals with my tendency to just start talking incessantly as well as you do." He kisses me lightly on the lips in reassurance, and we finally dig into our food.

Dax

AVA PARKS OUTSIDE the apartment building, her car idling loudly. "I told Noah I would take him sledding for his birthday tomorrow. He asked if you wanted to come along. Would you?"

"I have classes until eleven. Can we go in the afternoon?" Saying yes to going is one more step in the direction of a serious committed relationship. Ava and I still haven't defined what we are, but the more time I spend with her, the more I realize I want to claim her as mine. The knowledge that if Noah sees us together as more than friends means that Ava is telling me, without saying the words, that she is trusting me with more than her heart, but her family as well sits in the forefront of my thoughts.

I should be terrified. I should be taking this slow. That is the last thing I want. So far, following our instincts has worked in our favor, and I realize that I want more than anything to be a part of every facet of her life. Not just as her friend, but as her partner.

"Mom wants to do something in the morning, so the afternoon is perfect."

Kissing her goodbye, I reluctantly watch her drive away and hope that tomorrow afternoon comes quickly.

For possibly the first time in my life, I don't wake up when my bedroom door is opened. It's not until I hear Andie's voice getting closer to me that I finally realize it's not a dream. "Wow. You were really out. I just got a call from my lawyer's assistant. Apparently, the trial was bumped to today. She forgot to tell me last week, it's a good thing she called to confirm I would be meeting them beforehand. I need you there and that means you need to get up now."

Andie stays long enough to see me sit up before she races anxiously out of the room. "Shit." Running my hand through my hair, I'm thankful that Ava will understand why I need to cancel on Noah.

Searching my bed for my phone, I tap the button. Nothing. It was plugged in, why is it dead? Groaning as I see that I somehow pulled the cord out of the wall, I quickly dress and search for Andie's phone.

Dead also.

"What in the actual fuck? This can't be happening." Andie comes out of the bathroom, purse in hand. "Your car has a phone charger in it, right?"

"Yep. Ready?" Her voice is hoarse from her nerves.

Grabbing her arm, I pull her into a bear hug. "Hey, it's going to be okay. Once this is over you won't have to think about it any longer. Maybe he will finally get some sort of help; we both know he needs it."

She nods, handing me the keys to her SUV with a shaky hand. "Just don't leave my side."

"Is Lucas coming?"

She shakes her head. "He has a midterm today and then he is going to his parents for dinner to celebrate Noah's birthday."

She bends down to scoop up Luxe. Rubbing her cheek against his face, she takes a deep breath. Opening the door, I wrap my arm around her as she joins me in the hall. "Let's get this done with so you can finally move on."

Walking down the hall, I drop my arm and grasp her hand, squeezing it tightly. I've failed her in so many ways, I'm glad I can finally be where I need to be.

We've been driving for fifteen minutes when my phone finally turns on. "Will you please text Ava and tell her I can't make it this afternoon?"

"There is no signal. We will have to wait until we're closer to the city."

Tapping my fingers against the steering wheel, I grit my teeth and nod as I look at the time. I know how Ava is, and it's unlikely she will be checking her phone today, focusing entirely on Noah. At this moment, I wish she was more like other people her age and attached to her phone. Usually I love that she isn't, but I need her to know why I'm not coming.

"Oh! Two bars." Andie quickly types out a text explaining why I can't make it, reading aloud as she goes. "Shit, no bars again. Your cell service sucks. I never have issues along this road."

"My phone sucks, I think a demon possesses it and is laughing his ass off right now because I never have issues here either."

Andie reaches over, resting her hand on my forearm comfortingly. "Don't worry; we will make sure she knows."

I can't help feeling guilty that I'm so focused on my own shit when Andie is going through something actually important. I know Ava will understand, even if I don't get this sent to her. Yet here is Andie, comforting me. "I'm sorry. I'm being a shitty big brother."

"No, it's okay. You're distracting me from what is coming up. Although, I really need you to drive faster. You're going ten under the speed limit, and I don't have the patience for you to suddenly turn into a slowpoke driver."

Glaring at her, I speed up to ten over. "Better?"

"Much." She stares out the front window, chewing on her cheek as we get closer to Edmonton. "What if he gets out? What if they push it back, as we both know it's a great possibility? I just want this done. I don't want to think about it anymore."

"I choose to believe that it will be resolved today. Then you can move on. Remember when we used to think the world was so small? That we would be stuck in some never-ending nightmare? Despite that, you poured yourself into something productive. This will eventually be a very small black mark in an otherwise amazing life. I have no doubt that you will have everything you dream of." Glancing at her sideways, I'm relieved to see she is relaxing.

"I don't say it enough, but I admire you, Nugget, and you are a big reason why I am here now and not still making dumbass choices. You are my idol. You are who I strive to be like. Now let's show the world how badass you are and go in there with your head held high."

"I love you, Dax." Andie leans back into her seat and closes her eyes.

"I love you too, Nugget." She smiles at my nickname, her demeanor finally completely at ease.

As we get closer to the city, I fervently beg for today to move quickly and provide some closure for Andie. The words that I spoke to her also held meaning to me. So many of my choices have been wrapped up in the guilt I felt for not being able to protect her. Closing this chapter in our lives feels like it will finally allow us to move forward.

Maybe I will finally be able to forgive myself for allowing my anger to get the best of me for so long, giving me the ability to strive for a life I honestly didn't think I would be well-suited for.

My phone dings, notifying me that my message to Ava failed. Sighing, I look over at Andie. Getting her through this is more important at this moment. Knowing that Ava will be pissed off at me not showing up settles like boulders in my chest. One day I would like to accomplish not letting anyone down.

CHAPTER 10

Ava

CHECKING MY PHONE one final time, my heart breaks as there is still no contact from Dax. I've gone from worried, to pissed off, and finally settled on disappointed and heartbroken. This isn't just me he's standing up, that I could accept and get over, but it's the fact I told Noah he was coming and now I need to be the one to let him down. "I'm sorry Noah, Dax can't make it. He is really sorry." Noah's face falls, but he bounces back quickly. Most kids wouldn't be so accustomed to being let down by the men in their life. Thankfully, Lucas and my dad set a better example than the men I've chosen to have in mine.

"It's okay, Momma, we're still going to have a lot of fun." For a five-year-old, he is so resilient and understanding. I still can't believe my baby is five.

"Yes, we are. Plus we have to race and see if I can finally beat you!" Abandoning my phone on the counter, we finally make our way outside and to the large hill on my parents' property.

Noah gets onto his sled and waits for me to line up with him. "Ready . . . Set . . . Go!" He yells as he takes off, racing down the hill at a speed that I probably should be alarmed at. Giving him a head start, I slide after him picking up speed until I've almost caught up.

Noah sees me and shouts loudly. I slow down a little, letting him win. My sled starts wobbling and flips over causing me to tumble the rest of the way down the hill. Skidding to a stop, I gasp for breath as Noah's face appears above me. "Momma! You flew. Can I try that?"

"No! Absolutely not. Why don't I take some pictures of you sledding?" He races back up the hill with his sled and I sit up thankfully able to draw in a deep breath. "Ouch."

Digging my small camera out of my pocket, I snap shots of Noah racing down the hill. It doesn't take long to wear him out. After the fifth time down the hill, he drags his sled over to me and sits between my legs. "I love you, Momma."

Wrapping him into a tight bear hug, I tuck my face into his neck. "I love you too."

We sit like that until both of us are too cold. "Can I please have hot chocolate?"

"Of course." Noah whoops and jumps up, racing back up the hill, any tiredness disappearing at the promise of his favorite winter drink. I envy his energy. Despite the fun we've had, part of me was preoccupied with the man I am giving my heart to piece-by-piece. Anger surges through me, and I fist some snow into my hands. I will not be that girl. I will not wrap myself so entirely into a person again. I did that with Joe, and I refuse to lose myself.

No man is worth it. I want a partnership, a loving relationship but one that allows individuality. Scolding myself for not shutting off my brain to focus entirely on Noah, I throw the snowball and with it release all thoughts of Dax. I can deal with him later.

Pausing for one last look at Noah sleeping in his bed, I shut the door and make my way to the kitchen. "Thanks for making his birthday so special Mom. I think he had a great day."

"Good. I'm sorry you weren't able to fully enjoy it." She hands me a steaming cup of tea, gesturing to the living room.

"I didn't know I was so obvious. I shouldn't let something affect me so much. I think it was because once again I had to tell Noah that a man he admires is letting him down. It's not something I want him to grow up with. He needs to be protected; he needs only positive role models. We finally make strides with Joe and yet here I am introducing another inconsistent man into his life."

Mom shakes her head, tsking at me. "Ava, you can't hold Dax responsible for Joe's actions. This is his first transgression, and he may very well have a reasonable excuse. Everyone makes mistakes."

"I know you're right. I guess I just was disappointed as well. Is it crazy that I'm head over heels for this guy and until recently, we were only friends? I mean, I've known him less than six months. It feels impossible." My phone rings from where I left it in the hall. Ignoring it, I wait for her input. It took a teenage pregnancy for me to appreciate how wise she is and how valuable her advice is.

"Love happens in its own time. It took me three days to realize I loved your Dad. We're all different; we just need to learn to listen to ourselves through all the doubts and obstacles." She nudges me towards the hall as whoever is calling tries again. "Go. Listen. Process before your react."

Dragging my feet, I miss the third attempt and see it is Dax trying to call. I also have three texts from Joe. Wavering, I take the cowardly way and deal with Joe first.

> **Joe:** I hope you and Noah had a good day sledding for his birthday.
>
> **Joe:** I regret messing up my chance with you when I had it.
>
> **Joe:** All I ask is for one chance. One date.

Sighing, I hit ignore to another incoming call from Dax. Joe first,

Me: You had your chance. You need to respect my decision. Otherwise, we're going to have a serious issue. Why won't you accept what I'm telling you? This isn't you.

Joe: Fine. I guess everything I've done has meant nothing to you. Don't worry, I can do platonic ambivalence.

Me: Seriously? Now this I expect from you. If my decision not to be involved with you affects how you interact with Noah, you are gone from his life. I have no tolerance for inconsistency or bullshit.

Staring at my phone, I resist the urge to throw it when he doesn't respond. Typical Joe, he doesn't get his way and he shuts down. I'm just surprised it took this long.

Heading upstairs, I shut myself in my room and stare at my phone. I'm exhausted from dealing with Joe, but I know Mom is right. I know I would have heard him out, if I've learned anything in six years, it's how to face a problem head-on.

Leaning against my headboard, I return Dax's call. "Ava! I'm so relieved you called. I just got back to my place, I was about to jump in the car again. I'm so sorry for today, I tried texting, but I was having issues and then I needed to deal with something."

He doesn't give me a chance to say anything, so I wait for him to take a breath before I cut in. "It is fine, Dax. Relax."

"Fine? That does not mean fine in girl talk. That means you're pissed off at me. I truly have a good reason, I know you've dealt with this kind of shit from Joe, but this is different." His voice is low and I can hear him pacing around his apartment. Andie's voice fades as he walks away from her and gets louder as he walks towards her. Listening to the background, I'm pretty sure I hear Lucas shout in excitement.

"It really means I'm fine. What is going on over there?"

Hearing his voice makes my earlier anger and paranoia fade away. I trust Dax, I trust him more than I trust myself a lot of the time.

"It's a long story. This morning Andie came in. Her court date was moved to today, and she only found out this morning. I'm pretty sure the lawyer's assistant is going to be reprimanded tomorrow. She asked me to come with her for support, and I couldn't let her down. That's the only reason I didn't show up today." The background noise disappears and I hear a door close.

"Of course. I wouldn't expect you to ditch her for sledding. I was mad at first, but I trust you Dax. I know you will never not show up without good reason." Curling onto my side, I cradle the phone to my ear. It wasn't until I heard him say my name that I realized how much I missed him and hearing him talk has given me enough to last until I see him tomorrow. "How did court go? I'm hoping by what I heard in the background I'm about to hear good news."

"It's very good news. Dad got charged with assault. There was also a charge associated with his intent. The judge decided that without intervention, Dad would have killed Andie. He's on his way to prison, and the likelihood of him being released is low. We were in there for hours; he had a bunch of outstanding charges from trafficking, other assault charges, and theft. I don't think I've ever seen Andie so relieved as when she heard the judge's verdict." The happiness in his voice carries through the phone and I rejoice for Andie.

Getting off the bed, I put the phone on speaker and set about pulling out my paints. I need to use these feelings and put it on a canvas. "What a huge relief. She can finally put all of her fears behind her."

"Even better, Mom and Norman showed up. Andie's lawyer called Mom up to testify against Dad and she finally got justice for the years of abuse he put her through. We went out for dinner to celebrate." Shuffling rasps over the phone, Dax's voice sounding as if he's right in the room with me when he speaks

again. "I never believed anything like this would happen. I think we are all stronger for it."

"I think life has a funny way of testing you when you need it the most. I needed it when I was fifteen. You and Andie are stronger than any other two people that I know. I'm proud to have you in my life." The feeling of calmness that fills me as my brush dips into the paint, I stare at it for a moment before setting it aside. Dipping my finger into the paint, I go by instinct as I slowly fill in the canvas.

"I have so much more I need to say, but I'm being summoned to celebrate. I wish you were here." He calls out to Lucas, who's muffled voice comes through the phone so distorted I have no idea what he is saying.

"Of course. Go. I will see you in math tomorrow." His hangs up and I dive into my painting. It needs to be perfect to capture this moment. A moment worth hanging onto.

Dax

I'VE BEEN PARKED outside of Ava's house for twenty minutes. After hanging up with her and spending some time with the two lovebirds, I thought it seemed like a good idea to surprise her. Really, I was just disappointed that my afternoon with her and Noah was interrupted, even if it was for a good reason.

The front door opens, and I see Jules come out onto the porch. Too late to turn around now.

"I was wondering how long it would take before you finally came to the door, but it is too cold for you to sit out here. Go on up, Ava is in her room." She winks at me as I pass.

Stopping at the bottom of the stairs, I turn to look back at her. "Thank you."

When I open Ava's door, I see her sitting in the middle on her floor staring at a canvas. "I seem to have a habit of interrupting you while you are painting." She squeaks in surprise as she turns to me with wide eyes. Before she can get up, I'm on the floor pushing her onto her back. "I hated the idea of not seeing you today."

Closing the rest of the distance, I cradle her head as I devour her lips, the ache that has been building all day finally subsides. I've been so careful to be on my best behavior, my control around her is lacking. Right now, I can't think of why I thought it was so important to hold back.

Ava arches into me, responding eagerly to my assault on her mouth. Her hands tug on my hair; God, I love it when she does that. My body responds and she moans when she feels my erection against her hip. "Bed."

One word and I'm picking her up tossing her playfully onto the bed before making sure the door is locked securely.

My heart thuds as Ava slowly removes her clothing, laying back naked before me. Every inch of her is perfect. Scowling when her hands cover her stomach, I lean over the bed and move them. "Don't. Every single part of you is beautiful. Never hide from me."

Her hands fall to her sides and she licks her lips as I toss my clothes aside. I love that it's an unconscious movement; it makes her even sexier because she isn't forcing her reactions. They are real, just like her.

"I need you." The rest of my control evaporates and I lower myself over her, groaning as her hand wraps around my cock. My hips move with a mind of their own, finding a rhythm as I lose myself in her eyes.

"I love you." The words are out. It's the first time I've said them to a woman. Her hand stills as she looks at me, eyes wide.

"I love you too."

Crushing my lips onto hers, kissing her deeply ignoring my need for oxygen. My hands move over her body, worshipping every inch. Using one hand, I pin her arms above her head and tease her clit with the other. I need to bring her to her peak before I completely lose myself.

"You're so hot, so wet. I'm going to make you come so hard, you're going to have to bite me to keep from screaming." Her breathing becomes erratic as my fingers hook inside of her moving quicker and quicker until her eyes are squeezing shut with the effort not to make a sound. Putting pressure on her clit, I go harder until I feel her teeth sink into my shoulder as she reaches her climax.

Releasing her hands, I quickly sheath myself, filling her tight pussy. She's still pulsing, squeezing me tightly and I don't waste any time. Thrusting hard and fast, it doesn't take long to build her up again. My hands make their way back to her wrists, restraining her as I fuck her relentlessly.

Watching Ava have an orgasm is unlike any other experience I've had. Instead of immediately trying to seek my release, I revel in the blissed out look on her face, amazed that I put it there.

Ava pulls her wrists from my hands, gripping my hips and pushing me until I'm on my back. Hands planted on my chest, she moves her hips with a force that surprises and arouses me. My cock hardens more as I feel myself reaching the brink of my control. I love that she will tell me what she wants and take control. With her, I don't mind sharing.

My body shudders in pleasure as my orgasm rips through me. Ava moves harder as she tightens around me, leaning her body down to kiss me passionately. Our moans fill the room as we come down, bodies moving slower and kisses becoming deeper and less rushed.

"Stay the night." Ava whispers against my lips, her breasts teasing my chest as she rests on top of me.

"Are you sure? I don't want to cause any discomfort." I want nothing more than to stay and finally sleep with her in my arms for a full night. Waking up with her still there.

"You're staying the night." Her tone is firm as she gets off me, finding some sleep shorts and a tank top. "I need to find you something to sleep in."

She searches through her drawers before abruptly leaving the room. Disposing of the condom, I find my boxer briefs and slip them on just as she comes in with a pair of sweats I'm assuming are Lucas's.

"I hope these fit, you're a bit bigger than he is." Clasping my hand around hers, I tug her towards me, kissing her thoroughly before releasing her.

Pulling the sweats on, they thankfully fit decently well everywhere except the length. Ava rolls over from where she has laid down in bed and starts to giggle. "Men should not wear pants that show their ankles. Oh! I need my phone; I must take a picture of this. It's excellent bribe material." She reaches for her cell, laughing as I pounce onto the bed making her bounce.

Pinning her down, I wrestle her phone from her hand and set it out of reach.

"Not happening. You better be careful. Otherwise, you're going to be in trouble."

Her chin juts out, and she arches a brow at me. "Oh yeah? What are you going to do?"

Leaning down, I start nibbling on her neck teasing her in the ways I've discovered she loves. Moving lazily down her shoulder, I bite her gently grinning as she pants softly. Kissing my way up to the sensitive spot below her ear, I suck on the spot until she is moaning. Her hands reach up towards my hair and just as her fingertips tease the strands, I flop down beside her. "Goodnight." Pecking her on the lips, I roll over and close my eyes, waiting as she lays there in stunned silence with a grin so big it hurts my face.

I'm expecting her to say something, anything to get me to finish what I started.

I should know better, Ava rarely does what I expect.

Her breasts softly press into my back as her hand teases my hip, running a finger inside the waistband of my boxers.

Growling as my dick responds immediately, Ava laughs softly. Her fingertips are brushing against my skin in a feather light touch. My cock jumps eagerly as she runs a finger down its length, swelling as she grabs it in her fist and firmly brings her hand up to the tip. She releases me from her grasp and rolls over. "Goodnight."

Her body is shaking with laughter. She wins; she will always win just so I can hear her giggle. Flipping over, I wrap her into my arms pressing my arousal into her back and nuzzling my nose into her neck.

Her hand moves to slip between us, but I stop her. Holding her in my arms tightly. We don't say anything, our hearts falling into the same rhythm as we slowly drift off to sleep. She fits me perfectly, and I've never felt so content, so at ease with someone in bed with me.

CHAPTER 11

Ava

DISTORTED LIGHT SHINING through my curtains wakes me from a dreamless sleep. Dax's face, soft in sleep, greets me as I open my eyes. Smiling, running my fingers through his hair, I'm about to close my eyes again when I hear the thundering footsteps alerting me my alarm clock is about to burst through the door.

I wince as the door collides with the wall with a bang realizing I forgot to lock it. I feel rather than see Dax leap out of bed in surprise. Noah skids to a stop mid room, eyes wide as he sees Dax in my room with me.

This wasn't well thought out; I haven't even discussed Noah with Dax yet. Swallowing the shame I feel, I get out of bed with a calmness I don't truly feel. "Morning Noah." Ruffling his hair, I kiss him on the forehead. Noah has greeted me this way ever since he could walk, only missing it when Mom kept him busy so I could sleep in.

"Momma, can I bring my Nintendo to Show and Tell today?" Nodding, my heart sinks as he leaves the room without saying anything to Dax. A first for him.

"Shit." My knees are shaking, so I move back to the bed and sit down. "I'm so fucked up. I knew he would come in here, and yet it didn't cross my mind that we haven't even eased him into the idea of us and what that even means. We don't even really know what it means right now. We've had sex, went on a date, said I love you, and here we are. I'm okay with being unconventional, but this is out of control."

Looking up as Dax shuts the door, he's not looking at me as he responds. "Out of control?" My pulse pounds at the low tone in his voice.

"Everything up until this point has felt right. Things with you feel right and I could pour every ounce of my being into you. The thing is, I can't forget that with me comes Noah, and I won't let him be impacted negatively by this. I don't even know how you see yourself in Noah's life." Fisting the sheets in my hands, I watch his back move with his breathing.

Slow. Precise.

I know these signs, I've watched him enough to know that this is controlled and calculated Dax. The side to him I hoped I would never see in relation to me.

Yet when he turns around his eyes are vulnerable, and I realize that I have as much effect on him as he does on me. The fear he has at affecting Noah negatively is also apparent and for the first time I worry that fear will drive him away.

Stalking towards me, he sits down next to me on the bed, leaving a space between us. Noticing the look of hurt I'm sure is on my face he links his fingers with mine. "I have a hard time thinking clearly when I'm touching you," he explains. "Ava, the last thing I want is to impact Noah negatively. You're wrong, though, we do know what this is. We just don't need to have a long conversation about it. I want Noah to know we're together, more importantly, I want him to be okay with it. Let's talk to him about it. He's a smart kid, and there is no sense in trying to do this how others think we should, we've paved our own way so far, and it's working."

"Okay, you're right. Besides, I like that we are straying from the norm. That's how most of my life has been; it makes sense this would work out that way too." Standing, I pull him up and enfold myself into his body.

"A woman has admitted a man is right. This needs to be recorded." I can feel the grin on his face.

Glaring at him mockingly, I jab him in the side. "Shut up."

Moaning at the hand weaving its way into my hair, I almost forget what we need to do when he gives it a gentle tug. "Don't give me that look."

"You started it." Scrunching my nose when he laughs at my disgruntled tone. "Before we talk to him, I need to ask something . . . Noah is a permanent fixture in my life. He needs stability and consistency. How do you see yourself in his life? This has the ability to impact us and our relationship."

"Every moment of time I spend with that little boy, he ingrains himself further into my heart. I want to be a solid part of his life. I will be who you need me to be for him. I know that being with you means being involved in Noah's life and that is exciting to me." Watching him carefully, I see the sincerity in his eye and hear it in his voice. That's all I need to know right now, we can figure out the rest as we go.

Slipping my hand into his, I lead the way downstairs to talk to Noah.

We find him finishing breakfast in the kitchen. Smiling gratefully at Mom when she moves to leave the kitchen, I go and sit by Noah. "Are you excited for school today?"

"Yes! We have show and tell, and Mason said he is bringing his iguana. Can I get an iguana?" Noah's eyes light up with hope while I cringe at the thought of having a pet reptile.

"I think we should stick to furry pets, like Miss Andie's kitties." Taking a deep breath, I try to figure out how to tell a five-year-old about my dating life. "Before we leave for school I wanted to talk to you. I wanted to tell you that Mister Dax is going to be around more now. He is very special to Momma, and I hope that you're okay with that." Watching him carefully, I wait for a reaction.

"Okay. Mister Dax, did you see my Nintendo?" Noah doesn't wait for Dax to answer, he races out the door to grab his game.

"Well, I guess I made a mountain out of a molehill." Relief washes through me and I sink into my chair watching as Noah runs back into the kitchen and shows off his new toy. My phone vibrates and I see a text from Joe, apologizing for his behavior last night. Sighing, I type out a quick, forgiving, response. Everyone knows about Dax now except for Joe and since he is actively trying to be a decent father I know at some point that I need to tell him.

That's going to be fun.

The following week I still haven't had the courage to address my relationship with Dax with Joe. His texts are coming less frequently, but often enough that I know he hasn't let go of the idea of getting back together. Checking my phone, I smile at a goofy selfie from Kensi and Andie. It's been pleasant not dreading every time my cell notifies me of a text.

Tucking my phone away, I flip to a blank set of pages in my notebook and pick up my pen, idly doodling while I wait for class to start. I smile at Dean as he walks into class with Morgan on his arm, but it drops quickly when he starts to settle in the desk behind her instead of coming to his usual seat next to me. "Dean." Calling him, I gesture seriously when he glances in my direction.

"I know that look. What did I do wrong?" He grins at me crookedly.

"Dude, are you seriously ditching me for the guaranteed hour and whatever I actually get to see you to sit next to your girlfriend? I don't think so." Pointing at the seat next to me, I glare at him until he sits down.

"You're being a bitch."

"No, I'm not. I'm simply doing what you asked me to three years ago." He looks down in shame and I can't help but soften. "Are you taking care of yourself?"

"Seriously, Ava, I'm fine. Not the girl *I'm fine*, but actually fine. I've been feeling better for two years now and I think I'm finally over it." He avoids my gaze and quickly types something out on his phone.

"Depression isn't something you just get over. Please just take care of yourself. Are you coming to the game night this weekend? You should bring Morgan."

"I will be there." Dean smiles at something he reads on his phone. Sighing, I open my notebook and start jotting down notes. "Don't be grumpy. I'm sorry I was going to ditch you."

Unable to fight the smile at the ridiculous pout on his face, I shake my head. "You're lucky you're basically family. Remember, I'm watching you."

Relaxing as we fall into our typical banter, I push aside my earlier unease.

Dax

PEYTON IS ASLEEP on the couch, her books haphazardly spread around her, when I finally walk in the door after class. Smirking, I kick off my shoes and quietly walk to the couch before sitting on her.

"Argh! What the fuck?" Peyton's fist makes contact with my side as she kicks her legs until I stand up, laughing my ass off.

"I thought you were studying. I didn't realize that was code for napping." She tucks her legs under herself making room for me, and I sit next to her. Reaching down, I pile her books and place them on the coffee table. "It looks like you threw them on the ground."

"My head hurts. I have so much to catch up on, and I'm only doing two courses at a time. I thought I could get through them more quickly than I have been; I haven't even finished one yet. It's so frustrating, so yes, I threw my stuff on the floor and zoned out." Trying not to laugh at her rant, I nod empathetically. "Shut up. Not everyone can be as effortlessly smart as you are."

"I didn't say anything!"

"You didn't need to, I know you."

She rubs her eyes tiredly, causing me to grow serious. Eyeing her in concern, I see the circles under her eyes and the strain around her mouth. "I didn't realize you were struggling so much. Why don't you hire a tutor?"

"I can't afford to get a tutor. I need to get a job first. I will figure it out, don't worry. I guess I just thought it would be easier." Her head drops in her hands to hide the tears of frustration I know are forming. By the time she looks up, not a tear will have shed, and her eyes will be dry. It takes less than five seconds.

"Just take your time. Breathe. Remember it doesn't need to be completed overnight."

A soft knock distracts us as the door swings open, and Ava peeks her head inside. "Am I interrupting?"

"Not at all." Peyton jumps up, her demeanor changed like a switch was flipped. "We were just talking about my GED. Any interruption from that torture is welcome."

Ava shuts the door, joining us in the living room. Unable to contain the smile on my face as she sits on my lap and curls into me, my lips graze her cheek softly. "How was the rest of your day?"

"It was okay. Glad it's over." Ava turns to Peyton, trying to make sure she is included in the conversation. "I can't imagine how tough it is, trying to learn all of that material on your own. If you ever want help, in our group we have a math genius, a science nerd, a social sciences whiz and I'm sure any other topic you might need help with. Not that I'm assuming you can't do it on your own, I'm just saying you don't need to." Ava looks at me, her blue eyes cringing. "Why can't I just shut up?"

Before I can answer her, I see Peyton kick Ava in the shin. "Shut up? Why would you want to change who you are? Just roll with it, besides, that one there loves it, and I don't think any of us want to deal with him sulking if you quit saying the things you think."

Ava smiles gratefully at Peyton, an expression I can feel reflected on my face. Wrapping my arms around Ava, I revel in the fact my worlds have collided, and it hasn't been painful or scarring. In fact, it's been so seamless it's difficult not to wonder why.

"Are you still interested in having a painting day?" Ava's soft voice asks Peyton hopefully.

"Of course. I can't believe how quickly time has passed. Can we plan for a couple weeks from now, early to mid-March? I just want to get my bearings with these stupid classes."

"Definitely. I have midterms until March and this weekend I need to worry about Noah having his first sleepover with his father. It's been over a month, and I promised Joe we would give it a shot." Ava's phone vibrates, drawing her attention. "Speak of the devil. His ears must have been burning."

"I thought he wasn't bothering you anymore." Even though I know she has no interest, jealousy at the very thought of him pursuing her makes me annoyed every time he texts her.

"He still texts, less frequently, and almost always about Noah." Ava types out a response, hitting send. Before she has a chance to set her phone down it buzzes again. After the fifth message, Ava succumbing each time to whatever made up reason he's giving her to keep her attention, I can't take it anymore.

"Seriously, this needs to stop. He knows you have a boyfriend. He should respect you enough to stay within the boundaries you've laid out for him." Ava tenses, her chin dropping to her chest as she clicks her phone off. Watching her carefully, my instincts start roaring and I have to resist the urge not to remove her from my lap and force her to look at me. Clenching my fists, I look to Peyton pleading her with my eyes to leave the room. She gives me a warning glance before heading down the hall to the room she now shares with Andie. "He does know, right?"

I already know the answer, her body language cannot hide it. Ava is not good at keeping secrets, she has too many tells.

"No . . . I haven't told him yet." Whispered. Her shoulders hunch in as she waits. She can read me like a book, something I used to hate, but now I love. Most of the time.

"Why not? Should I be worried that you're entertaining the idea of getting back with him?" Inhaling deeply, I try to relax. That wasn't fair, and as I meet her eyes that are finally looking at me, I know she is pissed.

"Of course not. This is new territory for me, and I've been

trying to decide how to deal with it. He could make this very hard on us, and I just don't want more stress from him."

"Didn't it cross your mind to talk to me about it? That we could solve it together?" Biting back words I wouldn't be able to take back, I grab her wrists and hold them against my chest. "We said we were in this the whole way. Partners. That doesn't mean anything if we don't stick to it." My anger disintegrates as I feel her body tremble, and I pull her into my arms.

"I'm sorry. Why don't you come with me on Sunday when I drop Noah off for his sleepover, and we can tell him together?" Ava's breath teases my neck, coming in short quick bursts. "I love you. Please don't be angry. I'm still figuring out how to do this."

"I am too." Cupping her cheeks, I kiss her deeply. "I love you too. I think telling him together is a great idea, that way I can kick his ass if he gives you any trouble." Laughing, I pick her up and carry her to my room. "I think that was our first real fight. You know what that means, don't you?"

"Make up sex?" Ava bites down on my neck, giggling when the air hisses out from my lips.

"You better believe it." Slamming the door to my room, I drop her on my bed and show her exactly how fun making up can be.

CHAPTER 12

Ava

THE NOISE COMING from the living room muffles slightly as I stick my head in the fridge, looking for the platters of snacks Lucas and I cut up earlier.

"Can I help you with anything?" Hitting my head on the fridge as Peyton's voice pulls a shriek from me. "Oh shit, I'm sorry. I didn't mean to scare you."

Rubbing my head, I hand her a platter. She leans against the counter, staring out into the hall. "It's a little overwhelming isn't it?"

"Not the crowd. I'm used to being around a lot of people. It's more that everyone has this groove and I don't know where I fit in. With the Vipers, I knew exactly where I stood. I can see why Dax felt like he tainted the group." She plays with the cover on the tray, her voice soft as she talks.

"Neither of you taint the group. That's ridiculous. Besides, we've all been on the outside before. Just jump in and be yourself." Grabbing the other tray, I push her towards the living room. "Are we all set up in here?"

"We're just waiting on Dean." Lucas clears off room on the fold out table he borrowed from our parents for the food.

"We told you, man . . . he's not coming." Carter pulls the lid off one of the trays and grabs a handful of chips. "He said he's not feeling well."

Grumbling to himself, Lucas deals out the white cards. It was Andie's choice and she wanted to play *Cards Against Humanity*.

"Peyton, did you have a chance to meet everyone?" She shakes her head, and I glare at Lucas and Dax. Pointing at each person, I make sure I introduce him or her. "Kensi, Nella, Jaden, and Carter."

"Peyton, sit next to us. Seriously, I love your hair. I always want to do something like that, but with my delightful personality I figure it would be too much." Smiling gratefully at Kensi, I sit next to Dax and check out my cards.

"Have you ever played this game, Peyton?" Nella hands her a stack of white cards.

"No, I've heard about it before, but haven't played."

"Everyone gets a stack of white cards with statements, names, places; pretty much anything on it. The person who is asking the question draws a black card and reads it out. Each person picks his or her white cards with an answer or statement that is the funniest response. Then we go around the circle eliminating the ones we don't think are funny until only one card is left. The person who put that card down is the winner of the round. We play until one person has seven black cards. If you don't like your white cards, you can trade in a black card for new white ones." Nella explains the rules; Kensi is bouncing in place eager to get started.

Carter draws a black card and reads it out. Looking over my cards, I find the best option and lay it face down. It doesn't take long for us to start laughing our asses off. Kensi wins the first round, hopping up to do a victory dance. "Is that part of the game or more of your delightful personality?" Peyton teases Kensi who grins like a maniac.

"I like this one!" Kensi leans into Peyton and starts talking quietly with her.

"You seem distracted, are you okay?" Dax whispers as Kensi finally picks a card and reads it out.

"Yeah, I think so. I just have this feeling of unease, and it won't go away. I'm sure it's nothing." Leaning into him, I gently tug on the ends of his hair in the way he loves and smirk when he growls softly under his breath.

"Okay you two, we're waiting for you. Ugh, they're worse than you guys." Kensi points at Lucas and Andie.

Quickly glancing at my cards, I toss the first one and pick a new white card. The last white card is tossed into the pile and Kensi starts reading them out. I'm barely able to contain my excitement when Andie almost chokes as she laughs at my card regarding jerking off and churches.

Laughing so hard, I almost miss that my card is the last one standing. "Yes!" I yell, kissing Dax hard on the lips before leaning forward and drawing a black card.

"So how do you all know each other?" Peyton tosses her card into the pile.

"I went to high school with Dean, so he has known Ava and me for several years." Lucas answers, his forehead creased as he selects a white card. "Dean, Jaden, Carter and I all started the same year and met playing beer pong."

"I met Kensi after high school at the book store we both worked at. Nella and I met in the fall. And Lucas slammed a door in my face my first day here before I learned he lived across the hall. It was hate at first sight." Andie nudges him, grinning as she teases him about how much of an ass he came across as.

The evening passes quickly, everyone getting a little tipsy as the night progressed. Wobbling as I stand up, I grab another round. Nudging Andie with my toe, I tilt my chin towards Nella with a grin. Carter is watching her intently, looking away when he sees us watching and pulls out his phone.

It beeps in response to what he's just texted. "Well, as fun as this has been it's time for me to go." He stands, tossing his cards to the ground.

"Seriously, dude? We're in the middle of a round, you can't wait?" Lucas draws a card to replace the one he's laid down.

"I could, she can't." He holds his phone, cocky smirk in place.

"Ugh, disgusting." Kensi makes a vomiting motion, while Andie and I glance at Nella. She's never shown an interest in Carter, we just both want to see how she reacts.

"Whatever, ditch your friends to get laid." I grab his cards and stack them at the bottom of the piles. Nella seems indifferent, and that's all I care about. We don't always have power over who we're attracted to and the last thing I want is for her to stew in her own head over him.

Carter saunters out the door without a backward glance and we resume our game.

"Does he have booty calls a lot? I don't ever recall him ditching out on us like that before." Andie looks at Jaden, her question is casual, but Lucas gives her a weird look.

"I don't keep track of his movements, but he's been going out more frequently and at odd hours." Jaden answers, but I feel like he is being vague.

Finishing the round, Lucas and Nella are tied with six black cards; I change the subject from Carter to the shift in weather that is rapidly approaching. "It's supposed to be beautiful out in the next couple of weeks; we should plan a picnic by the waterfall."

"That's a great idea. It will be before the April crunch of studying for finals when we're all too stressed to leave the house." Andie turns to Peyton, "The trail system around here is stunning and there is this waterfall that will take your breath away."

Sitting there examining the cards as my friends make plans, I ponder the final two cards. Finally eliminating one, I look around to see who won the round.

"Oh! I win!" Nella exclaims. Kensi high fives her and rubs it in Lucas's face that he lost.

Standing and stretching, I start cleaning up the mess. Soon Dax is the only one left, his hands taking the garbage from me and pushing me towards my room. "Crawl into bed. We can finish this tomorrow after we drop Noah off."

Stripping down, I crawl into bed, my head hits the pillow, and the sweet darkness of sleep swallows me.

Dax

AVA TURNS DOWN a quiet street, slowing her car to a crawl as she drives down it. The duplex she parks in front of is neat, tidy, and looks like every other one on the block. "Is it just me, or is it creepy that every house looks exactly the same?"

The choked laugh that bubbles up is better than nothing, the grateful look she shoots me as she opens the door shows me how much my effort means to her. Shutting my door, I grab Noah's bag and stand at the hood of the car waiting while Ava unbuckles him.

Noah races to the door, banging loudly. "I should be happier that he's so excited. Joe has been consistent with his visits and FaceTime. Why don't I feel happier?"

"I think you're so overwhelmed with waiting for things to end badly that you haven't given yourself a chance to accept the way things are. I know I have that feeling on a regular basis. The waiting for something to take away our happiness." Her steps falter briefly as Joe opens the door, his eyes automatically dropping to our linked hands as he bends to pick up Noah.

"Daddy, I brought my Legos to play with. Can we build spaceships?" Noah's arms flail as he gestures excitedly.

"Of course." Joe looks away from us, his expression unreadable and sets Noah down. "Why don't you explore the house and find your room? I think you're going to like it."

The three of us watch as Noah races into the house. Joe turns back, leaning against the doorjamb, his arms crossed. He no longer hides his feelings about Ava and me standing on his porch, hand in hand.

132

"So, you two are an item now." He sounds tired, disappointed and for a moment I feel bad for him. He really had hope that Ava would give them another chance. "I guess I'm not surprised."

"I thought you should meet Dax again, in this capacity. He is a part of Noah's life and, therefore, a part of yours." Ava's hand squeezes mine. I can tell she's waiting for him to explode or fight her on me being in Noah's life. We had this discussion last night, how to deal with his reactions.

"He makes you happy?" Joe ignores me, staring intently at Ava, who nods in response. "Well, then we're good."

Joe turns away from Ava to stare me down. Fighting a smirk at his attempt to look tough, I wait for him to speak. "Noah's mentioned you almost every time we have a visit. He really likes you. Don't ruin it."

Managing to keep a straight face, I nod. "I won't."

"Want to see his room?" Ava nods and follows Joe into the house.

Thirty minutes later, we're back in the car and on the road.

"I thought that went well. He was surprisingly calm about us." Ava is grinning, her relief palpable.

"I'm not surprised, I told you last night he wouldn't react the way you were worried." I don't need to look at Ava to know she is rolling her eyes at me.

"Not this again."

"He's in love with you. At first, it was probably a fantasy after his family went through his father's recovery. But after spending time with you, seeing you with Noah and getting to know parts of you again, he's fallen. For him to react poorly would eliminate any hope he has that if things don't work out for us that maybe you will change your mind about him." Running my finger up her leg teasingly, I grin when she stops scowling. "What he doesn't realize is there is no chance of that."

"So what are you going to do to distract me from worrying

about Noah?" Ava's tone is suggestive, and while I'm tempted to bite the bait, I have another idea in mind.

"I thought I would tell you a bit more about my past. When I was part of the Vipers my job was a collector. The gang is one of the major drug providers in Edmonton, along with underground gambling and fighting rings. Ivan enlisted me to collect on debts. I used any means necessary to collect for him."

"The thing is, I wanted out. I wanted out for two out of the five years I was a part of the gang, but I just didn't know how. There was a police raid on one of the drug houses and I was in the vicinity when the gang unit busted us. They weren't able to find any association of me with the gang because I was very good at keeping my affiliation quiet, and Ivan didn't want to risk losing me. However, I did have some outstanding warrants and was arrested based off of them."

Taking a deep breath, I tell her something not even Andie knows. "I got out because that is part of my probation requirements. If they suspect I'm stepping outside of the law, I go to jail."

Falling silent, I'm surprisingly calm about admitting I was too cowardly to leave on my own. That I'm not truly the one to facilitate change in my life.

"It doesn't matter how you got out, what matters is that you're moving on with your life and doing an incredible job too." She reaches for my hand, her warmth never ceasing to amaze me. "How long is your probation?"

"I have two more years at the end of March. It would have been shorter, but one of my charges was escaping from lawful confinement. They want to ensure I'm reintegrated into normal society."

"You escaped from jail?" Ava's expression is shocked admiration. "I thought that only happened in the movies. I mean it makes sense that some people manage to do that in real life."

"I mean, I guess technically. It was a low-security facility, meant for those transitioning from different facilities and depending on why we were there, we were allowed day passes. I was only supposed to be there for a few weeks, but I left on a day pass and never went back." Shrugging, I know it's not something to be proud of, but four years ago, that was thrilling for me. Now, I look at my new life, and the thrill is finally having a life worth being proud of. Totally different, but much more satisfying.

"You really have led quite the life."

"How are you so calm about everything I tell you?" Tracing circles over the palm of her hand, I watch her drive, the slight tilt of her lips taunting me.

"Dax . . . Your past has helped mold you into who you are today. I love you, every part of you." She shivers, licking her lips as my fingers trail up her arm.

"I used to wonder what my life would have been like if I would have gotten out sooner, but then I might not have met you." Kissing her palm, I return to tracing soft circles on her hand. "Wow, I never thought I would ever say something like that."

"We all have that soft side and some people just need to find that person who brings it out in us." The look on Ava's face is mirrored in my own. We've run into this at full speed, there is no chance of looking back. We fall silent. I've noticed that as Ava and I progress in our relationship she feels more comfortable with us sitting and just being. The trees lining the road are a blur, brown ground starting to peak through the snow.

Reaching behind me, I fumble around for a couple bottles of water and granola bars. Twisting the top off, I hand one of the bottles to Ava. A sign on the side of the road distracts me. "Oh, pull off here. I want to show you something."

She signals and pulls into the turning lane.

"Keep driving and take your second left." Opening the granola bar, I take a bite, ignoring her curious glances.

Ava turns onto the thin gravel road, parking when we reach the dead end. "Okay, what is this?"

"You will see."

Leading her down a paved path, the trees thinning ahead to reveal a wooden platform overlooking vast wetlands. Ava walks to the railing, gaping at the sight before her. "Wow."

The massive moose moves slowly through the wetlands. "It was a long shot, but I heard about the place in my biology class last semester. It's a beautiful place and seeing the moose is just a bonus."

We stand in place watching him move through the wetlands. When he starts to move closer towards us, we make our way back towards the car, hand in hand. Looking down at the top of her head, I am awestruck that she thinks I am worthy of her and Noah.

CHAPTER 13

Ava

GLANCING AT LUCAS'S kitchen table, I try to organize my art supplies, so they look a little less daunting. Peyton is supposed to be here soon to paint with me, and I know how overwhelmed I was the first time I realized just how much more to art there is than simple brushes and paint.

Recalling standing in an art supply store staring at all of the different mediums, I'm excited to introduce Peyton to the fun she can have without needing the end result to be perfect.

Out of the different types of paintings I do, mixed media is my favorite. The abstract products made from any tool you can think of are fun to create, and you can't go wrong. Layer upon layer until you feel like it's complete.

A soft knock followed by the door opening alerts me to Peyton's arrival, and I turn, eager to see her reaction. Grinning as she gapes at the supplies, her reaction is exactly what I was expecting.

"I think you're mistaking me for someone who knows what they're doing." She creeps closer, intimidated by the spread before her.

"Don't worry, I know exactly how you feel and I can

guarantee by the end of this afternoon you will feel differently." Gesturing to one of the chairs, I sit across from her. "Okay, let's jump right in."

Scanning the table, I pick up a bottle. "This is called gesso. We start with that because it primes the canvas. You don't need to use this every time, but for the purposes of getting comfortable, we will use it. Now, I like to put it on sporadically. It doesn't have to cover every inch of the surface, by leaving some parts of the canvas uncovered it changes the way the paint looks in those areas."

She picks up a paintbrush, stopping as I laugh and shake my head. Wiggling my fingers, I pour some paint onto my mat and start spreading it over my canvas with my fingers. Peyton lays her brush down and follows suit.

"I have to admit, I thought I finished finger-painting after elementary school. This is fun though and more soothing than I thought it would be." Peyton finishes spreading paint over her canvas. "It's a good thing I don't mind getting dirty."

Smirking at her innuendo, "It's probably a good thing the guys aren't here. They would have a field day with that one."

"They really are an interesting bunch. You wouldn't think their different personalities would mesh so well."

"They have a good balance."

Watching as Peyton covers her canvas, I admire how well she seems to accommodate to any situation. "This is relaxing. I can see why you do it."

"I paint any overwhelming feeling I have. It helps me process. Most of them I give away, but I do have a stash of really personal ones I'm saving for when I have my own place." Handing her a dryer, we sit silently listening to the whir as we watch the gesso dry. Turning mine off, I run my hand softly over the canvas and nod to Peyton.

"Okay, so I typically use acrylic paints." We select our colors, and I'm impressed when Peyton chooses different colors than I do.

"How's your GED going?" As I show her the steps, I take the opportunity to get to know someone who means so much to Dax. She's been staying with Dax for almost two months and I don't know her that well.

"It's still challenging me. I think I told you I'm only doing two courses and I still have several more. I dropped out halfway through grade ten. I have over two years to make up. So many regrets." Her hands stay busy, mixing paint and adding layers.

"I don't believe in regrets. It would be so easy to get lost in them." Peyton gets up and washes her hands. Grabbing a Sprite, she gestures and hands me one when I nod.

"I wish I had your optimism." She takes a deep drink of her Sprite, before picking up a stamp pad. "It's kind of been ingrained into me to be skeptical."

"You and Dax both." She laughs. "Although, he surprises me a lot of the time, he manages to give me a perspective I often miss. We've been dating for a short time, even though it feels like we've been together forever because he knows me so well."

"He's shockingly intuitive for a man. I love it and hate it because he will never sugarcoat things." Peyton shakes her head, smiling fondly as she remembers something he must have said to her once.

"No, not even with Noah. He always tells him the truth." We laugh, and I find that time is passing quickly chatting with her. I adore our group of friends, but there is something about Peyton that draws me in. She gives off an aura of loneliness, and that is something I can relate to.

Several hours later, Peyton proudly holds up her canvas as Dax, Lucas, and Andie come in the door. The three of them stare incredulously at her, and even I have a hard time holding back a chuckle.

"Did you use your face to paint?" Dax gestures at smudges of purple paint on her chin and left cheek.

"Shut up. Ava made me use my hands, and I had an itch." She elbows him in the side as she walks by towards the kitchen sink, spinning around and swiping her thumb across his cheek at the last second. Dax growls playfully before they both head to the bathroom to wash up.

"Before this turns into a paint fight, we need to finalize our plans for this weekend. We've been pushing back our picnic all month, and we finally have a window of nice weather. The snow is almost gone, and it might be our last chance before we're all killing ourselves prepping for finals." Andie helps me tidy the kitchen, making room for everyone to sit done.

Dax and Peyton come back from the bathroom, paint washed away. Dax beelines it for me, leaning down to kiss me. "Hi, Sunshine." The simple nickname makes my whole body react, right down to tingling in my toes.

"Hi. Where were you today?" Smiling up at him, I ignore the chorus of groans around us.

Ignoring my question, he turns back to the group. Jabbing him in the side for being avoidant, I turn my attention to the conversation going on around me. Andie and Lucas just found out that Dean is planning to bring his new girlfriend. I'm the only one who has sort of met her and since they started dating; he hasn't been around as much.

"I know I give Dean a hard time for being a player, but I already hate this chick. He doesn't even sit with us when we share a break the way he used to. He's changed; he's not as easygoing and doesn't laugh the way he used to." Andie scowls as she talks. She and Dean became surprisingly close early in the year when they found they shared a class, but she still doesn't know about his history. "He hardly talks to me in class anymore. She's changing him and not for the better."

"He still sits with me in class, but that's because I gave him shit." I don't hate Morgan, but I definitely think they need more balance. Especially Dean.

"Let's be supportive and wait to make a judgment for after we meet her." Lucas wraps his arm around Andie. I know he is also worried about Dean, I can tell by the tone of his voice, but like me, he is ever the optimist. "He's been texting me, and he seems happy. He's coming to the picnic because I gave him hell for not having more balance and he agreed that he may have gone overboard."

We move into the living room, Andie loading Mario Kart onto the screen. She looks around hopefully that someone will join her, bouncing excitedly when Dax and Lucas grab controllers.

Peyton comes to sit next to me, "Don't you play?"

"Against Andie? No. She's insanely good, and I'm not. It takes me at least two rounds to figure out the controls and even then I'm lucky to beat Lucas."

"Hey!" Lucas shouts at me indignantly, shrugging when Dax passes him leaving him in last place.

Leaving the room, I go into the kitchen to start cooking dinner. We tend to rotate whose house we eat at; Andie, Lucas, Dax, Peyton, and I are the frequent diners. We're joined less often by Jaden, Carter, and Dean.

"Ava, thanks so much for today. I would love to do it again." Peyton starts shredding lettuce for a salad.

"Anytime, just send me a text." Handing her the rest of the veggies, I pour marinade over chicken breasts and slide them back into the fridge.

We finish prepping dinner in comfortable silence, something that would have been impossible for me at the beginning of the semester. Letting my thoughts drift, I think about all the ways my life has changed in the past seven months. Smiling to myself, I finally don't feel like I'm missing out by not traveling and painting. I was meant to be here, to realize how full my life could be while still being able to enjoy my passion.

Today was incredibly fun teaching Peyton different techniques. "I think I'm going to change my major." The words pop out of my mouth before the thought is even complete.

"Really? To what?"

"Teaching, with a minor in art. Why I never thought of it until now, well I don't know. All I know is all I've ever wanted to do is be creative, and that will allow me to have a reliable career with art still part of it." Spinning around, I hug Peyton.

"What was that for?" Startled, she awkwardly pats my back and I step away before I make her completely uncomfortable.

"Today, teaching you. That enabled me to see how I could combine what I want in a job and what I need in a job. I don't think I will ever be able to thank you for that."

Peyton stands there, shock on her face that she could impact someone so positively. It makes me want to hug her again, but I refrain.

Sticking the potatoes in the oven, I mentally note scheduling an appointment with the registrar's office. Things are falling into place, and I don't ever remember being happier.

Dax

WE'RE IMMERSED IN an epic game of tag, Noah racing away from Carter to escape being "it." Everyone has joined in while we wait for Dean and Morgan to show up so we can eat.

Ava races over to me and I leap out of her reach having lost track of who is "it," right into the path of Jaden, who I missed while chasing her. "Boom. You're it." Jaden races off, grinning like a fool.

"Hey, guys." Dean says as he walks over and sits on the blanket spread out close to the waterfall, a petite blonde at his side. "This is Morgan."

Morgan smiles shyly, and we abandon our game, Carter flinging Noah over his shoulder and running in circles to distract him.

Ava sits down with them, talking quietly and pointing out everyone to Morgan. Sitting behind Ava, I pull her into my chest. "Hey, dude, it's been too long."

"I know, I've been hearing about it from Lucas. My brother got admitted to the hospital last week." Ava is watching him carefully, her brows creased.

"Morgan, would you like something to drink?" Ava gestures to a cooler several feet away. They get up and walk together, chatting. Morgan seems like a nice girl, quiet but not withdrawn as I expected. Watching as the other girls join Ava and Morgan, I turn to Dean.

"What happened with your brother?" Dean doesn't watch Morgan the way I expect him to, with how preoccupied he's been with her. The shadows under his eyes are concerning and now that my attention is focused on him, I notice he's lost a ton of weight.

"He has bone cancer. He was diagnosed four years ago and went into remission two years ago. He fell skateboarding and broke his wrist, when they scanned it there were dark spots in the bone. He had been having pains and suspected the cancer was back, but didn't tell anyone. He's only sixteen. Not only am I angry, but I feel helpless, and that's not a feeling I deal with well."

"Wow. I'm sorry to hear that, I know it doesn't make any difference, but I am. Sometimes you just need to get out of your head, even for a moment. Why don't you come out with me and Lucas later, get your mind off things?" I know that going out is probably not on his priority list, but I also know that dwelling on things you can't change doesn't make it better.

"Yeah, I guess it's better than sitting at home." He looks up as Ava and Morgan sit back down beside us. Morgan hands him a drink, leaning into him and whispering softly. He smiles, whispering back.

"Morgan was telling me how she wants to run her own preschool. She's graduating this year and has even found a space. It's too bad she didn't have it for this year, I could have sent Noah to her." Ava smiles warmly at Morgan, whatever reservations she had about her gone.

"I'm sure that there are enough parents in the student body here that you could inquire with the university. Maybe they will give you a better rate than in Jasper." Trying not to react at the surprise in Morgan's eyes at my suggestion, I'm thrown back into feeling like I don't belong. The look is gone in a flash, and I'm sure the surprise is more that I would think of something like that, but my insecurities of not belonging have resurfaced.

Noah calls me over to where he is playing a game of catch with the Jaden and Carter. Kissing Ava on the cheek, I get up to join them, relieved to be doing something. The way my brain works is so fucked up.

The smell of burgers on the grill makes my stomach growl. "Mister Dax, your stomach sounds like it has a bear in it."

Noah presses his ear to my stomach as it roars loudly. "Well, so much for playing catch. Apparently your stomach is more interesting." Carter tosses the ball in the air, migrating toward where Lucas is grilling.

Soon we're all sitting on the blankets eating; Ava curls next to me, not engaging in the chatter going on around us. "What's wrong, Sunshine?"

She leans into me, her lips tilted downwards in a rare frown. "It's Dean. I thought, hoped even, that he was distancing himself because of Morgan. I was talking to her and they're not spending as much time together as we thought. With his brother coming out of remission, I don't think he's handling the stress well. He just needs us to be diligent in dragging him out."

"He's coming out with Lucas and me later. We will knock some sense into him." She frowns at me, and I soften my face to show I'm kidding.

Ava relaxes as Dean starts to join in, laughing as Carter teases him about hiding Morgan for so long because he was scared she would trade him in.

"So I have some news . . ." Ava looks up at me, her expression serious. "I should have said something sooner, but I wanted to be sure everything would work out. I've decided to switch my major to education. I realized when I was teaching Peyton how to paint how much fun it was and realized I could teach art."

Her face breaks into a brilliant smile, her excitement palpable. "That's perfect for you! I knew you could find a way to do what you love for a living." Wrapping an arm around her waist, I brush my lips softly against hers, smirking when she moans with need. We shift a little, turning our focus back onto the conversation flowing around us.

A grape hits me square in the forehead, a muffled giggle betraying Peyton as she lobs another grape. Picking it up, I crush it between my teeth, enjoying the pop of the skin and the tart juice. Picking up the other grape, I throw it back at her and manage to get it down her top. "This is nice" she mouths at me.

Looking around our group of friends, I nod. "Beats the Vipers." Mouthing back, she smiles happily and joins the girls in a conversation about waxing. Silence falls around us as Kensi reenacts her reaction to getting a Brazilian. Cringing, I look at Lucas and scrunch my face. "We need to pack this up before they start talking about periods."

Laughing, we tease the girls as they huff impatiently.

My phone dings notifying me of an email. Checking it, I fist my hand to prevent an audible reaction. I'm not ready to share the news; I want to see how it goes first.

CHAPTER 14

Ava

THE CRUNCH OF gravel beneath our feet is the best sound I've heard in a while. The snow is almost gone and even though that means finals start in a couple of weeks, it also means more time outdoors. Noah releases his grasp on my hand when he sees the playground ahead with Lucas racing after him.

"How's my big brother treating you?" Andie bumps into me, laughing when I stumble. "Whoa! Even the mention of him is sweeping you off your feet."

"Shut up. It feels insane to be at this point already, but I guess love doesn't really have a timeline. People may think I'm naive, I just know we make each other better." The words sound cheesy and Andie smirks at the ridiculous smile on my face, but as she looks at Lucas chasing Noah around the playground, I know she understands.

"You know I get it. Sometimes the people we think are the opposite of what we want are exactly what we need." She links arms with me, leaning in to whisper, "Lucas asked me to move in with him. Err, you guys."

"What! That's fantastic!" Lucas turns, brows arched at my squeal.

"Now that I know you're on board we can make an appointment with housing. Thankfully they are pretty flexible." Andie does a twirl; she's been so much more at ease since her father was sentenced. Laughing, I join her causing Lucas and Noah to stop playing and just stare at us.

"When are you going to tell Dax?"

Andie groans, chewing on her lip. "I don't know, we haven't spent a ton of time together between our relationships and Dax starting his job."

"Wait. What? Dax has a job?" Grabbing Andie's arm, I jerk her to a stop, cringing as she almost falls from the force of my pull.

"Shit, I can't believe he didn't tell you. He started a couple of days after our picnic, working the evenings you're at home with Noah." Andie kicks the sand as we sit at the picnic table, watching Lucas help Noah with the monkey bars.

"He never mentioned it. I've noticed he isn't as chatty those nights, but I never thought anything of it. Why wouldn't he tell me? What's the job?" My heart throbs at the hurt I feel that he would keep this from me. I thought we were past the point of secrets.

"Parkland was hiring students to paint the areas they've been renovating, the hours are flexible, and the pay is decent. I thought about applying too, but I would rather get a job at the library or in Jasper." Andie weaves her fingers together, a sure sign she is agitated. "I don't want to be the cause of problems with you two, even if it is his fault for not telling you."

"I'm not mad at you. I'm not even mad at him . . . Not really. I don't understand why he wouldn't tell me, since we've all been talking about finding part time jobs." Smiling at Andie, I try to ease her worry. Instead of dwelling, I wink at her and race off towards Lucas and Noah. She quickly follows, laughing as Noah hangs upside down making monkey noises.

"Where is Mister Dax?" Noah's face is getting red from being upside down, so Lucas helps him down.

"He is busy today. What, is Uncle Lucas not being as fun as Mister Dax?" Ruffling Noah's hair, I laugh as Lucas tries to tickle my sides.

"No, Uncle Lucas isn't as fast." Andie and I burst out laughing as Lucas stands there stunned. Noah is bent over laughing at his own joke.

Lucas throws Noah over his shoulder, running in circles as Noah laughs until he's red in the face. Dropping to the ground, Noah rolls away trying to catch his breath. "You're still slower."

"I can't win with this kid." Lucas sits on a whale statue. "Andie told you our news?"

"Yeah, she's pregnant." Andie coughs and turns away, covering her mouth to hold back her laugh. Biting down on my tongue, I barely hold my straight face as Lucas freezes.

Sputtering, he makes sounds that no one would be able to translate. Finally, we can't hold in our laughter. "Yes, I told her."

"Not funny."

"It was funny." I sit next to him on the whales head, punching him hard on the shoulder. "C'mon. Don't be mad."

Standing, he wraps an arm around me. "I'm not. Now how long do I have until Noah gets picked up by sper . . ." Elbowing him in the side, he notices that Noah is within earshot. "I mean . . . Joe picking up Noah?"

"Any minute. I guess his company is willing to transfer him to their branch in Hinton so he can be closer to Noah. He's taking Noah to look at some apartments. That means we could shift his overnight visits to when Noah and I have school because it would be close for him."

"Are you sure he only wants to be closer to Noah?"

"Yes. He's been on his best behavior since I told him about Dax."

"Good." Lucas rests his chin on Andie's shoulder, kissing her below the ear.

The sound of a horn honking draws our attention to Joe

parking his vehicle next to Andie's SUV. Noah runs to greet him, the three of us following more slowly.

"I'm glad Noah has a relationship with him, but I still hate him." Lucas's face is set in a scowl, no attempt on his part to hide his distaste for Joe.

"Wipe that look off your face, for your nephew's sake." He plasters a fake smile on his face, and strides forward toward Joe.

"Hey, man. How's it going?" Sighing, I go to my car ignoring the show Lucas is putting on. Grabbing Noah's bag, I toss it into Joe's car and help Noah into his seat.

Andie drags Lucas away, scolding him for being an ass. "Well, I see he knows how to let go of a grudge." Joe's voice is tainted with sarcasm, but when I turn to look at him his expression is filled with humor.

"Yeah, he has trust issues." If I'm honest, I'm still waiting for Joe to slip up in his act and show his true colors. Andie says that trauma changes people, whether it's for the good or not is up to them.

"I guess I don't blame him." Joe smiles wryly. "Well, I better head out. I will let you know when I find a place so you can come and check it out."

Watching them drive away, I turn and smack Lucas, who is leaning against Andie's car. "You need to get over his behavior. I have. People change, and they can change drastically and quickly. You know this as well as I do." It's a low blow, but he has the grace to look ashamed.

Wiping the paint from my hands, I abandon my current project. None of the layers are turning out how I want them, and I've painted over the canvas entirely in black. My meeting with the registrar's office this afternoon went well. In September, I will officially be an education major with an art minor.

Joe found an apartment, and it's perfect for him and Noah.

Everything is falling into place, but my mood is foul. I don't even know why I'm so grumpy, but something is not sitting well with me today. Lucas and Andie left in a hurry when I got mad at Lucas for the TV being too loud.

Slamming the bathroom door, I silently chastise myself for taking out my bad mood on everyone and anything. I even snapped at Dax this morning when he left for class. Cranking the water until it's running hot, I shed my clothes and glare at myself in the mirror. It's been ages since a mood like this has hit me. The last time was right before I found out I was pregnant. Refusing to believe that's the reason today, I step into the shower and try to figure out what else it could be.

The hot water runs over my shoulders, doing nothing to ease the tension. Going through the motions of my shower, I finally make the decision to take a test. It won't hurt, and at least I can eliminate that from the reasons behind my mood. Typically, when I get this unreasonably angry, it's because my head is telling me something is wrong, and I'm in denial. I just need to face it head on.

Turning the water off, I text Nella. Out of all of my girlfriends, I know she is the least likely to spill the beans. I'm barely dressed, my hair in a knot at the top of my head when there is a knock at the door.

"Ava?" Nella's voice startles me even though I'm expecting her.

"In the bathroom." Shaking, I listen as her footsteps get closer. She silently hands me the box and shuts the door behind her. Fumbling with the box, I mentally prepare myself for the results. How could I let this happen? We've been so careful. Shutting my brain off, I focus on the task at hand.

Opening the door, I slide down the wall next to Nella. "Now we wait."

"Ava, you're basing this off of your mood, not even your cycle. Just breathe." Nella reaches over and holds my hand. Resting my forehead on my knees, time passes too slowly, but the time to check arrives too quickly. "Okay. It's time."

Standing shakily, I go back into the counter and flip the pregnancy test over. The words are right there—*not pregnant.* "Oh, thank God."

The idea of having another child, a child with Dax whom I love, is something I want. In the future. Once we've been together for a long time, finished school, found employment. Crying in relief, I hug Nella. "I told you. You're probably upset because Dax hasn't told you about his job and you're holding it in. Go, talk to him and your mood will improve."

"I know." Throwing the test in the box and tying it in a bag, I'm grateful when Nella takes it from my hands. Maybe she's right; I'm just upset that he feels the need to keep a ridiculous secret from me. That's no reason to be so angry about it, but I hate secrets, and I hate holding things in. *Stop acting like a child.*

Dax

ZONED IN ON the TV screen, I don't look up as Andie comes in from her workout. I'm kicking ass in Diablo 3, something I haven't been able to focus on in weeks.

"Mind if I join you?" Andie collapses onto the couch, taking the controller I wordlessly hand to her. "Where is Ava?"

"She's at home painting. She was in a foul mood this morning, and I think she wanted to clear her head. I've never seen her so grumpy, but I guess we all have our days. It was kind of cute, but she got even more pissed at me when I told her that." Andie loads her character into the game, and we take off on the next quest.

"Yeah, she's got a lot on her mind what with Joe moving to Hinton and . . ."

Pausing the game, I turn to look at her head-on. "Since when is Joe moving to Hinton?"

"He found an apartment there last week. His company is transferring him to their branch in Hinton so he can be closer to Noah. Wow, you guys need to work on your communication skills and that's coming from me." Andie resumes the game, carrying the weight of my character as I digest the information she's just told me.

I know I haven't told her about my job, but that's only because I wanted to make sure it worked out. This is more serious than a job, though. The more I think about it, the more irritated I get. Why would she keep that from me? The pessimist inside wants to go to the worst possible scenario.

Andie looks over her shoulder at the door when it opens.

Eyeing me as she sees who it is. Without looking, I know it is Ava. Normally I would be jumping over the back of the couch, but I'm so agitated I take the low road and keep playing until Andie shuts down the X-Box, and leaves the room with an emphatic look at me.

"Joe's moving to Hinton? When were you going to tell me?" Keeping my voice low, I know the scowl on my face has brought men to their knees. Ava gets in my face rather than cowering, another thing I love about her. "You are such a hypocrite! When were you going to tell me about your job? Why does it matter if Joe lives closer to his kid? It's not as if he's moving in with me, in fact it works better because it will save me driving time and I will have my days off with my kid. I didn't say anything because it's not a big effing deal. Just like I didn't pick a fight over you not telling me about your job because I figured that wasn't a big deal. But since we're discussing secrets, how about you admit you might not always be as direct as you say you are." Floored by the volume of words that have flown out of her mouth, I start laughing. Doubling over when she gapes at me in shock.

"I'm sorry it's not funny. You're right, I should have told you. And it's not a big deal that he lives closer. My suspicious nature took over and turned off the rational part of my brain. I want to know these things though, because you and Noah are important to me." Reaching out, I pull her into my lap. "I should have mentioned the job. I just wanted to make sure it worked out. I can't stand the idea of you ever being disappointed in me."

"Impossible." She straddles me, silencing anything I was going to say, as she owns my lips. Moaning when she cups me through my jeans, I lift her and carry her to my room. Ava doesn't waste any time, pressing herself into me as I walk. Setting her on the ground, I quickly strip away her clothes.

"Get on the bed." My voice is demanding, my cock standing at attention as she obeys. Quickly removing my clothes, my eyes wander her body. She no longer tries to hide the silvery white marks on her stomach, her eyes simply aroused as she waits for me to take charge. I love that she will command what she wants when she wants it, but I can demand what I need in return.

Moving over top of her, I roughly grip her hips and thrust inside her tight, hot depths. Taking her hard and fast, I love watching her eyes as she builds up to the point of orgasm; the way they become hooded the closer she gets almost as though it's too much for her to focus on keeping them open. As she clenches around me, I flip onto my back, carrying her with me until she is riding my dick. Gripping my shoulders like a vice, she moves her body forcefully, taking from me what she needs and giving me everything I want in return. As I feel her body tighten around me, I sit up, fisting my hand in her hair and pulling until her neck is exposed. Biting down before trailing hard kisses over her throat, my orgasm rips through me as she continues to ride me.

"Perfection." The word sends a shudder through her body. Blue eyes lock with mine as I release her hair, her hands reaching up to tease the strands of my hair while we silently gaze at each other.

"Next time I'm in a piss-poor mood, pull my hair and fuck it out of me. So much better than how I spent the day." Lifting her off me, gently laying her on my bed, I laugh softly.

"Oh, I love it when you talk dirty to me." Sitting next to her, I stroke my fingers over her stomach, grinning when she flinches away as I graze her ticklish spot.

Ava captures my hands, telling me all the ways she wants to torture me when I tickle her. Her smile is mischievous as she wrestles me down, her naked body towering over top of me, gloriously beautiful. Letting her pin me down, I try to remember what it was like before her, before I was this happy. The memories are there, but the sting has faded. She has shown me what it's like to be accepted wholly for who I am.

"That's a crazy idea." Realizing too late the words have been spoken out loud, her eyes questioning as she waits for me to elaborate. Breaking free of her hands, I buckle her hands until she's flush with my body. Her warm skin is sending pulsing shivers throughout my nervous system. Cupping one side of her face, I watch her gulp nervously as I waver over if we're ready. Going with our instincts has worked so far. "Marry me."

Her eyes widen in shock, before a smile breaks across her face, and she nods.

"Say the words."

"I will marry you."

Pulling her head down, I lose myself in kissing the woman I never want to live without.

CHAPTER 15

Ava

WAKING UP IN Dax's arms the next morning is surreal. Outwardly, nothing has changed, but inside my entire being feels like it is glowing. Two years ago, if someone had asked me if I thought I would meet *the one* before I turned twenty-five, I would have laughed. Now as I feel his chest move, hear his heart beat underneath my ear, I know it is right for us.

Running my fingertips along his chiseled stomach, loving the way his abs flex beneath me, I try to wake him up slowly. Resting my chin on his chest, I watch as he sleepily opens his eyes, the happiness from last night filling them as he focuses on me.

"Good morning, Sunshine." Leaning my head into his hand as he runs his fingers gently through my hair, I wish we could stay in bed all day.

That thought is cut off as my alarm goes off, reminding me that we need to pick up Noah. "Good morning. Are you ready for a day at the zoo?"

"A day with you and Noah? Always." His eyes light up as we discuss the plan for the day. His love for my son is apparent as he speaks about him, not that I've ever doubted his affection.

"So, I've been thinking." Focusing on pulling my pants up, I don't meet his eyes when I feel him turn to look at me. "I don't think we should tell anyone quite yet. I want to get through finals before we spring this on everyone."

I finally look up when he doesn't say anything, holding his gaze as he searches my face. "All right, I guess that makes sense."

"You're not angry with me?" Whispered words show the fear that I've upset him. His arms wrap around me, holding me firmly in place as he buries his face in my hair.

"Of course not."

The zoo is more of a discovery park with animals. The setup is more open than a zoo, focusing on creating realistic environments for the animals, all of which have been rescued and rehabilitated. There aren't as many animals as there would be at the Calgary or even Edmonton Zoos, but the experience feels like more because you get to see the animals as they journey through their recovery.

"Momma, can we see the bears first?" Noah grabs Dax and my hands as he drags us in the direction the picture of a bear is pointing. Grinning at Dax as he stares in wonderment where his hand joins with Noah's, I swear I see a sheen to his eyes as he quickly looks down the path. This side of Dax is one that only a select few are privileged enough to see, most people only get to see a guarded version of who Dax truly is.

Noah drops our hands as we arrive at the bear exhibit. Both grizzly bears are lumbering about, close enough that you can see their enormous size. As one stands on his hind legs, Noah grips the railing to stand on his toes to see them better.

Dax bends and picks Noah up, setting him on his shoulders. Stepping into his side, I slide my fingers into his and squeeze.

Standing there, watching the bears, it feels like we are already a family. The picture of what I had always dreamed of is no longer hazy. These are the moments in time that we often forget to cherish and as Dax squeezes my fingers almost as though he knows what I'm thinking.

"Momma, are you and Mister Dax going to get married?" Noah's question causes me to choke on an inhalation. Bent in half, I laugh at the irony of his timing.

"Why do you ask?" Finally able to form words, I look sideways at Dax who is smirking as I deal with this question. I don't want to lie to Noah, but I know we need to inform Joe before we tell him.

"Ben at school has two dads and I thought it would be cool if I had two. Plus then when I'm with Daddy, you won't be lonely." My throat catches at his concern for me, Dax's hand squeezes mine, grounding me.

"You don't have to be worried about me being lonely." I fumble around my head trying to think of how to distract Noah from his initial question, thankful when the bears start playing and distract him from my lack of an answer.

Glaring at Dax as he chuckles softly, he shows no shame as he teases the skin around my left ring finger.

Moving on from the bears, we circle the entire park, stopping at each exhibit and watching the animals. Dax buys us all some caramel popcorn. The entire time we walk through the zoo, Noah stands between us, holding both of our hands.

We spend the whole day at the zoo, revisiting our favorite animals and picnicking by the elephant so we can watch her bathe herself. This entire day will be imprinted in my head; the first day we've spent together knowing we will be a family. Knowing that these kinds of days, these adventures are just beginning. Some people wait their entire lives to start living, all I needed was Dax to show me I could do what's best for Noah and still have a part of me that is more than a mom. A person independent in herself and capable of handling whatever comes.

"Let me drive." Dax holds his hand out for the keys to my car, and I gratefully drop them onto his palm. "I've been thinking about selling my motorcycle. Now that it's spring, it should go fairly quickly. It's not very practical when it's my only vehicle, and I figure it's time I start thinking ahead."

"Dax . . . You don't need to do that. I know how much you love that bike." Twisting in my seat, I face him square on.

"Honestly, it's something I've been thinking about for a while. It sucks borrowing Andie's vehicle in the winter. Besides, I can always buy a new, better bike down the road. It's not forever, just for now, but keeping you and Noah safe, that's forever." He glances at me before focusing back on the road. "I hope that doesn't eliminate my bad boy status though, I wouldn't want you second guessing our relationship."

The muscles in his forearms ripple with tension as he grips the steering wheel. This is the only outward sign that he's only half-joking. "I don't think that's possible. You will always have that vibe about you."

Shifting so I'm facing forward again, I watch the blur of the trees fly by. Eyes drifting closed, I smile when Dax folds my hand in his. Safe. He always makes me feel safe.

Dax

THE BOX FEELS heavy in my pocket; my hand obsessively checking to make sure it's there. Knowing how I made the money in my savings, I only momentarily thought about using any of it for this purchase. Instead, I listed my motorcycle on the University's buy/sell Facebook page. It sold that same day. Leading me to where I am now, laying in Ava's room waiting for her to get home.

Today, I made one of the most important purchases of my life. It should have been exhilarating, or at the very least held more excitement than it did. However, it was entirely uncomfortable. The saleswoman was obviously uneasy with me, and I hated being in that store. There were over five sales representatives, all dressed up in designer clothes, all looking at me with varying levels of disgust or nervousness. Watching every step until finally one woman lost the draw and had to help me.

I would have walked out. I should have walked out, I almost did when I saw the ring. To me, it was perfect. A single oval diamond circled with delicate sapphires the color of my eyes.

All the discomfort in the world was worth going through to find this ring. I just hope she feels the same way.

I don't have to wait long before I hear Ava come in the door. Faintly, I can hear her moving throughout the apartment. Abandoning her bags in the living room. Perusing the fridge in the kitchen. Every second that passes is torture.

Finally, her footsteps echo as she walks down the short hall. She gasps as she sees me in her bed, hand clutching to her heart. "Holy crap. You gave me a heart attack."

"Not the first time someone has said that to me." Smirking, I hold my arms open waiting for her to join me on her bed.

"I thought you had to work today." Her warmth presses against me, momentarily distracting me from the anxiety I've been fighting with.

"They let us out early. Apparently the board of directors for the University is taking a tour of the renovations." My hand folds over the small box in my pocket. Wavering over what to say, I give up trying to think of something and silently remove it from my back pocket.

Ava's eyes are closed, only opening them when I turn her hand over and set the box on her palm. Watching her nervously as she stares at the box, I resist the urge to snatch it away. I hate feeling vulnerable and out of everything we've gone through, this is in the top three vulnerable moments. To some, it's just a ring. To me, it's a symbol of what my life has become, the person I've become and it rests on the finger of the woman who made it possible, where it will stay for the rest of our lives.

Her eyes move quickly between the box and me, before she silently closes her hand and draws it to her. She slowly sits up, every movement feels like it takes longer than it should. Holding my breath as she opens the box, my heart stops at her intake of breath.

She just stares at it.

Seconds tick by, no movement.

"Dax . . . It's . . . Perfect." Her hand shakes as I remove the ring and slide it onto her left ring finger. Breathing out a sigh of relief as it slides on smoothly.

"I know we're not announcing anything yet, but I couldn't wait to give it to you." She turns her hand back and forth, looking at the ring on her finger.

"Maybe we can tell Lucas and Andie. It's been torture keeping it from them." Almost as though they heard Ava say their names, the door to the apartment opens carrying their voices down the hall.

We join them in the living room, Ava bouncing excitedly.

"What's going on?" Lucas looks between us humorously, jaw dropping when Ava thrusts her hand out, the ring on full display.

I've only heard Andie squeal a handful of times, but the noise coming out of her as she rushes Ava has me eyeing the window for cracks. "That noise is going to shatter the window. I'm pretty sure I hear dogs howling outside. Are you excited, Nugget, or summoning the wolves?"

"Shut up. Oh, my freaking . . . When?" Andie inspects the ring before hugging Ava tightly. "Nicely done Dax." She moves to me, hugging me forcefully.

Lucas is slower to stand, and I straighten as he approaches. It never crossed my mind that he might think it's too fast or disapprove. Shit, I didn't even ask Ava's dad for his blessing. The excitement of the moment fades as I dwell on my fuck up. My mind slowly processes the smile on Lucas's face as he hugs Ava before clapping me on the shoulder.

"From making out in the hall to being engaged in a matter of months, I can't say you guys are traditional." He winks at me, and I finally relax.

"It is fast, but it feels right. You are the only two that know, please wait until we announce it after finals." Ava tucks herself back into my side. "We don't have a date and most likely we will wait until at least one of us is done with school."

Andie chatters excitedly about how that gives us more time to plan the wedding. I gape at her even more as she pulls Ava into the kitchen. She's changed so completely, in all the ways I hoped she would as she started to truly deal with her issues and I realize that I've done the same thing.

Lucas chuckles as he pushes me towards the kitchen. "I just heard the words 'destination wedding' you may want to get in there."

Hurrying into the kitchen, I laugh as Andie blushes guiltily. "It's just a suggestion."

"Why don't we get through finals and then you can figure out ways to spend money we don't have." Elbowing her in the side, I sink into a chair.

"Bullshit. I know you have a savings account full. Enough to replace your bike and pay for a nice ceremony." Andie smiles triumphantly.

"That money is tainted. Besides, that's how I'm paying for school." Ava and Lucas watch us curiously. Sighing, I explain. "I received a percentage of whatever money I recovered for Ivan. Since my expenses have always been small, until starting school, I put most of it away. Part of me always felt guilty for having it. I'm not proud of the way I got it."

Lucas looks confused as I speak, but Ava's expression is understanding.

"We have time. I'm not in a hurry."

The four of us sit at the table, talking about how much has changed over the past year. The train finally feels like it's moving the right direction down the tracks. Looking towards Andie, we smile at each other. Genuine, at peace smiles. A cycle we both dreaded is finally splintering into a million possible directions.

CHAPTER 16

Ava

UNABLE TO BEAR the thought of taking my ring off, I switch it to the other finger. After telling Lucas and Andie, keeping it a secret no longer seems as important as it did a week ago, but every day I switch my ring to my right hand.

My first final is in twenty minutes, and I'm already sitting in the empty classroom pouring over my notes. Slowly the room fills, Dean appearing right as the exams are being handed out.

He's a mess.

"I was at the hospital all night. The treatments have been making Danny really sick and I wanted to be there for him." He fumbles around for a pen, groaning as he comes up empty handed.

"Here." Handing him my extra pen, I rest my hand on his forearm. "I'm sorry about Danny. Maybe once finals are done, we can visit him and have a game night. Take his mind off what he's going through."

Dean gives me a small smile, but it doesn't reach his eyes. A test lands on the desk in front of me, stealing my attention. I wish we were anywhere but here. Dean may not be the one going through chemotherapy, but he needs support too. Shame fills me as I realize I've been so caught up in Dax that I haven't even really checked in on Dean since the picnic. The only thing that brings me comfort is knowing how involved and supportive his family is. Maybe that's all he needs is to be surrounded by them, regardless of how sad the circumstances are.

That thought easing my guilt, I immerse myself in my final. My first semester of university is coming to a close. People always say you change during university, I just never expected so much so fast.

Handing in my exam, I decide to hit the library for some quiet study time. Finding a quiet corner, I sit on the floor and surround myself with my notes. My next final is in Art History, and while I know most of the techniques they discuss, some of the actual artwork tends to slip from my brain.

"Psst. Ava." Suppressing a groan, I look up as Kensi folds herself up into my tiny corner. So much for studying.

"Hey. Don't you have an exam right now?"

"I'm done."

Looking at the time on my phone, I gape at her. "You finished in under thirty minutes. How is that possible?"

"I have a strict policy with exams. I always do best when I work through them as quickly as possible. That means I don't have time to question myself." Kensi has always seemed rash; everything she does has instant gratification in mind.

"Whatever works for you." Stacking my notes, I lean into the corner. Out of all the girls, I'm the least close with Kensi. I'm not surprised she came to say hi, but I am surprised she is lingering this long.

She fills the silence with whispers of parties she has heard about and her plans for the summer. Apparently, her parents are forcing her to spend the summer on Vancouver Island with them. "It's not that I mind going, I know this is their way of guaranteeing they see me before I disappear during the new school year again, I just will miss you guys."

Thinking about my first summer with Dax, I feel the smile

creep up on my face. "Sorry, I'm not laughing at you being kidnapped for three months, I'm just thinking about Dax." Unconsciously my fingers play with my ring. Kensi's sharp eyes notice the movement, her hand darting out to grab my right hand.

"Holy shit! And you didn't tell us?"

"We wanted to wait until after finals." Smiling as I gently remove my hand from her grasp, I answer the string of questions she fires at me. No sense in trying to keep anything from her, she is relentless when she wants something.

What feels like hours later, she leaves me back to my studying, and I know it's only a matter of minutes before everyone else in the group knows about the engagement. Flipping through my notes, I sigh happily as I set my alarm for when Dax gets off work.

Dax

COVERED IN PAINT, I finally walk into my apartment and beeline it straight to the bathroom. It feels incredible to wash away the sweat and dust. The construction manager asked if I would be interested in learning how to drywall. It pays an extra few bucks an hour, but I always leave covered in a layer of drywall dust. The water finally starts to run clear, and I turn the tap off.

Despite picking up close to thirty hours of work this week, I've written two of my five finals and don't feel like I'm drowning. I think it would be impossible not to be optimistic, every time I look at Ava my world is complete.

Toweling off, I toss my dirty clothes into the hamper and quickly throw on the first clothes I find in my drawer, regretting that decision as I realize the jeans have a hole in the crotch and the t-shirt is actually Andie's.

Starting over, I finally feel like a normal person.

Grinning when I hear the door to the apartment open, I go to join Ava in the living room.

Turning the corner, I pause stunned before the rage fills me. Peyton sits on the couch, quietly sobbing, while Ivan and Tom sit on either side of her. Tom's arm rests over her shoulders and I see red. "Remove your arm before I remove it from your body."

Tom's face whitens, he was always a pussy, and his arm falls limply to his side.

"Now now, Dax. No need for hostility." Ivan's voice is placating, having the opposite effect of what he's hoping for.

"What the hell are you doing here? Peyton, are you okay?"

She shakes her head, fresh tears rolling down her face as her breathing accelerates to near hyperventilation.

"Breathe Peyton. This can all be fixed, as long as Dax is willing to help."

My jaw hurts from clenching it so hard, and I have to focus on unlocking it. "I ask again, what the hell are you doing here? What is going on?"

Peyton stands, her voice trembling. "It's Bear. Manny has him."

Peyton's brother Bear is two years older than I am, the one who Peyton followed into gang life and the closest member of her family. Understanding why Ivan and Tom are here dawns on me. "You want me to get him."

"Manny likes you, we're willing to pay the price, but he won't let any of us close." Pacing the room, my mind reels. The chances that Ivan is full of shit are high, but the risk if he's being forthright isn't one I'm sure I want to take. Peyton's eyes plead with me, Ivan and Tom promise it's a quick job and then they will leave me to my boring, menial life. Nodding, I quickly jog back to my room to grab my wallet and cell phone.

When I get back to the living room, Ava is standing there frozen and wide eyed. "Dax?"

Her voice is soft as she asks the question she can't put words to.

"We've just met your lovely girlfriend. While I regret we don't have more time for pleasantries, we need to hurry, our window is only so wide. Shall we?" His tone is pleasant, but I can see the joy behind watching me trying to stay afloat.

Dismissing Ivan, I ignore his smirk as he and Tom vacate the room. Peyton waits anxiously by the door, all thoughts on Bear and not about the look on Ava's face.

Realization.

"You're leaving. To go with them." Her words are sharp, causing me to cringe, which just affirms what she's already been told.

"Peyton's brother Bear is in some trouble, and I can help." I try to convey the importance of why I'm making this decision to here, my words pleading her to understand.

Her face closes off, disappointment the only emotion she's letting me see. "You promised. You told me when we were sitting in the car that you were done with that part of your life. That you had no interest in EVER going back. When you proposed to me, and we lay there talking until the early hours of the morning; all that talk about priorities. Was it all bullshit?"

"I'm not going back for good, I'm just going back to help Bear." Stepping towards her, I freeze when she steps away from me. "I know where my priorities lie, Ava. If I thought there was another way, I wouldn't be going."

"No. You made me a promise, one you can't break every time something happens. You think this is the only time? He's found a crack in your resolve, and he's going to use it." Her voice stays low, breaking with the feeling behind her words. "Your head is clouded and he's manipulating your fear."

"It's for Peyton." Pleading. Begging her to understand, hoping she won't let this ruin us.

"I love Peyton, but you need to choose. Your future with me, with Noah. Or risking everything to hang onto a past that will continue to suck you back in whenever you show weakness. They will continue to use Peyton against you, and that's her family, she will let them." Her words cut me like a knife, I look at Peyton over my shoulder, her tears have stopped and have been replaced with a look of determination. If Ava's words sting, she gives no indication. When I look back at Ava, the only person in this room that she sees is me. "Please, Dax. Please don't go. We have a life here, a future. Please . . ."

The thickness of her voice cuts me as I see her struggling not to cry. The words, *please don't go* flooding from her at a rate so fast they blend together. I'm not even sure she sees me anymore, her body seems smaller than it is as she continues to ask me to choose her.

"She's family, Ava, please don't make me choose." Reaching for her again, I watch as her face breaks, the tears flowing freely down her cheeks.

"You've already made your choice, and I can't be involved in it. I won't put my heart through this again, and if you're willing to go back once, I can't trust you won't go back again. I can't do it to myself, or to Noah. What if you didn't come back? There is more at risk here, and you know it." My eyes drop to her hands, shattering my soul as she slips off the ring I gave her only a short time ago. "I love you. Goodbye, Dax."

My hand is limp as her trembling fingers set the ring inside it, squeezing my hand tight around it before falling away.

My throat seizes as she slips past Peyton out the door, both of us cringing when the door across the hall slams. Peyton's eyes are wide as I walk past her and down the hall, her feet rushing to catch up as I bound down the stairs without looking back.

"Dax . . ." Peyton stops me before we exit the apartment, the realization of what I'm sacrificing for her breaking through her grief. "Go back there. Tell her you made the wrong choice. I shouldn't have asked this of you, knowing you would never say no. You can fix this, I can try to help Bear, and Manny might talk to me."

Pushing past her, I don't respond. I've already done the damage, hurt Ava in a way I promised myself I wouldn't. Ava's face is all that I see as I get into the vehicle. It's all that I will see the entire four hour drive to Edmonton. It was as though I watched her heart break, my feeble hope that she would understand why I was doing this shattered as she handed me the ring.

Staring out the darkened windows, I watch the door hoping to see her. When the building disappears, I set my phone on my lap, hoping to see her name.

It never comes.

There are moments in life that we regret, but we're able to

live with. Watching as I was the cause of her breaking, that is something that will torture me for the rest of my life. Something I will never forgive myself for.

Tucking my phone away, I harden myself. I find the person I thought I left behind and I cling to the heartless, cold person I know I can be.

CHAPTER 17

Ava

DROPPING THE SPOON into the ice cream carton, I abandon it on the floor at my feet. It didn't help me feel better. Cradling my stomach, I breathe past the pain that waves through me. It's been several hours, and he hasn't come into the apartment to tell me he made a terrible mistake. I'm not surprised. One of the things I love about Dax is how protective of his family and friends he is, but to go back into that world is something I cannot handle. The pain of losing him would only be surpassed by the pain of him being hurt, or worse . . . killed.

Curling more into myself, I don't bother looking up as the apartment door opens. I know it's not him.

"Hey, Ava." Andie greets me as she pulls her shoes off, filling me in on the brutal exam she just took. She turns from hanging her coat up and pauses mid-sentence. She sees the puffiness of my eyes, the empty ice cream carton at my feet. "What happened?"

My face falls as she looks at me with concern, her eyes so like Dax's. "Dax and I broke up."

Shock fills her face, and she stumbles towards me, collapsing on the couch. "What happened?"

The last thing I want to do is relive earlier this afternoon, but I fill Andie in anyways. My voice cracks as I try to explain how Dax chose to leave even though I asked him not to, but the wound is still fresh. "I'm sorry, this is too hard. I can't talk about it anymore."

Andie reaches out and takes my hand, squeezing it tightly. "I'm calling him. I can't believe he would go back. I'm half tempted to call the cops and let them know where they can find Manny."

"You can't. He's in breach of his probation by going." The hand around mine tightens causing me to flinch.

"Probation?" She hisses out a breath, momentarily distracted from my pain. "I guess I should have known. I mean he always had . . ." She breaks off as she focuses on the grimace on my face.

We sit silently. I'm too exhausted to feel awkward, her hand firmly holding mine. Shivering, my body feels like I've been run over by a bus. Andie reaches behind me, covering me with a blanket.

"I'm going to make you some tea." Nodding blankly, I watch as she casually tries to pull her phone out. Rolling over to face the back of the couch, I pretend in my head that I don't hurt so badly. When that doesn't work, I allow myself to hurt until tomorrow, and then I need to toughen up. This is why I told Dax I couldn't let him be my entire world. Andie returns with a steaming cup of peppermint tea, my favorite, and sets it down on the coffee table when I don't turn over.

"Andie, I love you, but I think I want to be alone right now. Sort through this in my head, maybe paint a little once I can. I'm only allowing myself tonight to be sad. Tomorrow I need to be a mother, a student, a daughter, and a friend. I need to remember that I am a whole person outside of my relationship." Andie nods wordlessly, handing me my tea as I sit up.

"Please text me later. I'm sure it's not easy being around me, but regardless of what my jackass of a brother has done, nothing changes in terms of our friendship." She waits for me to acknowledge what she's saying, staring at me until I finally nod.

The door shuts behind her, the sound is loud in the silent apartment and causes me to flinch. Sipping my tea, I try to remember that I am not the same girl I was before Noah was born. I let myself fall apart when Joe ended things and even though this hurts a million times more, I'm not going to be so weak.

Heaving myself off the couch, I migrate to my room. The black canvas I abandoned so long ago sits on my easel. Setting my tea down, I reach into my bin of paints and grab the first tube my hand touches. Soon the familiar comfort of painting lulls my head into a safe and comforting place.

Reaching for my brushes, I catch sight of a photo of Dax and me. I'm laughing at something he said, neither of us is looking at the camera only at each other. Abandoning my painting, I take the picture off my nightstand and sit on my bed.

My door slowly opens, Lucas stepping in cautiously. "Andie told you, didn't she?"

Nodding, she comes and sits next to me, looking at the picture in my hands. "I didn't believe her at first, but it's a little late for April Fools." He leans back against the wall, grimacing at his attempt at a joke.

"I didn't think this would happen. I thought we had forever. Was I unreasonable for making him choose?" Lying back on my pillow, I wait anxiously for Lucas to respond. I already doubt my decision, wondering if I acted rashly.

"No, I don't think so. It's not something you want to be associated with and if he's drawn back once it's not impossible to think it might happen again." We sit silently, the photo still in my hands. Lucas takes it from me, looking at it before setting it aside. "I guess I just wonder how you will feel about it tomorrow, or even next week."

"What if I didn't walk away now, giving him the benefit of the doubt that it was a one-time thing and then six months from now there is a new disaster? We had the discussion! I thought I was clear about where I stood, and he still chose to go. He watched me walk out the door and left with them." My voice reaches a high level, eyes burning as fresh tears threaten to spill. "This hurts and every moment since I left the apartment I've been second guessing the decision to end things. I begged him, Lucas, I begged him not to go. Pleaded while he stared at me. I saw the torture in his eyes, but I also saw the decision he made. I don't think I could go through that again."

"Okay. I told Andie I was going to stay home with you tonight, what do you want to do?" He smiles at me brightly and my lips twitch in return. It's not a real smile, but I appreciated his effort.

"I don't want to do anything."

He nods in understanding. "Okay. I will make us some dinner."

Left alone, I curl onto my side. I know that eventually the feeling of hollowness will subside, that the ache in my chest will ease.

Time passes in a blur; it feels like I've been lying in bed for hours when Lucas calls me for dinner. He means well, making sure I get up and move around, and it's difficult to drag myself up, but once I'm at the table, I feel grateful to be doing something normal, something that doesn't remind me of the tears in my heart.

"I don't know if you want to hear this, but Andie texted me to let me know Dax is okay. He and Peyton are on their way home." Nodding, I quickly glance at the clock on the microwave, shocked at how much time had passed.

My heart flutters in relief that he's okay, and then stutters at the apprehension of realizing I will be running into him regularly. I forgot about that.

Dax

IVAN STOPS OUTSIDE the grungy house, turning towards me expectantly. "While you're in there . . ."

"You've got to be fucking kidding me." Leaning into his face, I stare him down as I make myself clear. "I am not your pawn. I am here for Peyton and Peyton alone. This is a ONE-TIME thing. I go in, retrieve Bear and get out. After this day, you do not contact me and you do not contact Peyton. Otherwise, you will be on the receiving end of the wrath you've never thought twice about using." Ivan is not one who usually shows fear, but he's never had my rage fully unleashed on him and at this point I have nothing left to lose, and he's aware of that. Gulping, he nods and turns back to the front of the car.

"Don't move, this isn't going to take long." Exiting the car, I stalk towards the house.

Two men greet me, searching me before letting me enter. Ivan isn't wrong, Manny does like me, but that doesn't mean he trusts me, especially with Ivan parked at the curb.

The house is quiet and surprisingly neat. I don't hear or see Bear as we make our way to the backyard. Once outside, my eyes automatically survey my surroundings, noting where everyone is located, and quick escape routes. This habit is not one I've shut off since leaving the Vipers, and it's one I think will stay with me for life.

Realizing that Manny is having a party, I hope that my promise to be quick will be kept. A few people by the house are snorting cocaine, completely ignoring the guards and me as we pass. A girl is on her knees in front of one guy sucking him off.

Disgust fills me as I recall when my evenings were spent in crowds like this.

Finally, I spot Manny in the back corner of the yard. He sees me standing there and gestures for me to wait, finishing his exchange with the gentleman facing away from me. The guy slips out the back gate after handing Manny a package.

Manny saunters towards me casually, a friendly smile on his face. He's a prime example of a guy who makes bad decisions, but is completely likable if you don't know what he's capable of.

"Dax! It's so good to see you, even if you did leave that scum tainting my front yard. How are you?" He slaps my hand, giving me a half bro hug.

"I'm fine. Honestly, I just want to get this exchange done so I can get back to my life." I try to maintain a level of respect in my voice, I'm not really pissed at Manny, it's the way this world works, and if Bear was crossing boundaries it's his own fault he got caught.

Manny nods sympathetically. "I don't know why he got you involved, I told him we could do an exchange elsewhere, but you know Ivan. He wanted to punish you for leaving, what better way than to use your attachment to Peyton."

Seeing red, I realize that everything Ava told me was right. How she has a better grasp of the way Ivan thinks than I do is beyond me. I completely fell into his trap. "Why did I not see it? I've watched him do this to countless others."

"You're too close to the issue, and that's why you were never meant for this world. Don't get me wrong, you're amazing at what you do, but you form attachments. Real attachments." Manny gestures behind me. "They're bringing Bear out. He only has some minor injuries; it didn't take long to realize he was just being a dumbass."

Nodding, I'm still caught up on how easily I was manipulated. The rage that had finally started to simmer boils up. "I think my ego just got too big, I thought he would be too intimidated to try something like that with me."

Bear stumbles out of the house, looking relieved when he sees me. Examining him with a clinical eye, I only see some faded bruising. Turning back to Manny, my mind calculates how I can exact revenge on Ivan. "I've always liked you Dax, so I'm going to say something completely uncharacteristic. Don't. Do. Anything."

"Here." Handing him the envelope, I ignore his request. Turning on my heel, I exit the back yard, grabbing Bear's arm and dragging him through the house. He doesn't say anything, smart enough to know I'm ready to smash his face through the wall and break his arm. When we get to the car, I unleash the rage.

Grabbing the back of Bear's neck and shove him up against the car. Ivan, Tom, and Peyton stay in the vehicle, held in place by the twisted look on my face. "Here is how this is going to go down. You either get your shit in gear so I never have to save your punk ass again, or I will bring so much pain that you will wish I just killed you. Do you fucking hear me?"

The whites of Bear's eyes circle the irises they're so wide. Gulping, he silently nods unable to speak because of the grip I have on his throat. Releasing him, I watch him cough to relieve the pressure my hand caused on his throat. It's disgusting, but that sound makes me smirk.

Stalking around to the driver's side of the car, I open the door and yank Ivan out. He puts up a fight, only satisfying my need for violence more as I kick his feet out from under him and smash his head on the pavement. Grasping his hair, I pull his head up and slam it down again, the satisfying crunch of his nose breaking only fueling me more.

"Listen here you piece of shit. Manny happened to inform me that he offered to meet you in a neutral location, and you refused. You have only managed to piss me off. See, I was perfectly content to live my life and completely forget about the Vipers, but now . . . Now I have nothing to lose." One of the car doors opens, and I shoot a warning glance, thinking it is Tom coming to Ivan's defense. Peyton's cautious eyes meet me instead.

Turning away from her, I press my knee into Ivan's back. "If you ever and I mean ever threaten anyone who is important to me, past, present or future, I will make your life hell. I never want to see you or even hear your name again." Twisting his arm behind his back to make my point, I lean down growling in his ear. "I have people ingrained in your system. A simple phone call and I can have you gone. Just remember that."

Peyton's hands are on my shoulders, pulling me back. The world is hazy, blurred by the rush I've always felt doing this. The release of anger, instilling fear in people. "Dax, step away. Remember who you are, not what you've done."

A crowd is building on the lawn, Manny standing on the porch watching with thinly veiled interest. "You're right. He's not worth my time." Standing, I swiftly kick him in the side before taking Peyton's hand and walking her back to the house. Bear follows silently at a safe distance. "Manny, do you mind giving us a ride to the west end? I have something I need to pick up, and I think my ride is no longer available."

Manny gestures to his second in command, if I recall correctly, his name is Rich. Nodding at Manny, I leave Ivan behind without a backward glance.

It's not until the car is moving that what I've resorted to sinks in. The coldness melts away and the person I've become fights his way to the surface. Telling myself I did what I needed to do, I fight the shame.

Peyton's warm hand finds mine, squeezing it gently. "Everything will work out."

All her words do is remind me of what I've thrown away.

CHAPTER 18

Ava

COLLAPSING AT THE kitchen table, I grab an orange and start peeling. Everyone has been by my side for the past few days, hovering to make sure I'm okay even though they know I'm not. All of my energy is spent being the mom and student I need to be, crumpling at the end of the day in a heap of exhaustion. Sleep still evades me.

Wearily standing after I devour the orange, I stumble my way to the couch to try to sleep. Being in my room is difficult, the memories of so many moments with Dax spent in there. The painting I finally finished a taunting reminder of how it felt when he let me walk out the door.

Covering my head with a blanket, I focus on tensing and releasing my extremities in an effort to relax my body into sleep. My eyes begin to feel heavy, and I'm hopeful that it's working when the door opens. Sighing as my brain clicks back on, I lift the covers to see who has come into the apartment.

Peyton shuffles her feet awkwardly, as though unsure she will be welcome. I can't even be angry with her; if our roles had been reversed, I would have asked for the same thing. Hugging the pillow to me, I nod towards the empty spot at my feet.

Her eyes are shrewd, and I can't help but chuckle darkly. "I know, I look like a member of the Addams family."

She sits on the edge of the bed, the frown on her face never lifting. "I'm so sorry, Ava. I should have known better than to ask Dax that. If he had no idea what was going on, you would both still be happy."

Her eyes are fixed on her lap, her voice soft with guilt. Struggling to sit up, we both laugh real laughs when I get tangled in the blanket and almost fall off the couch. "I don't blame you. If the roles were reversed, I don't doubt I would have asked the same thing. I just couldn't sit back and watch. Forever it would be at the back of my mind, waiting for the next time. I can't do that to myself and especially to Noah."

Her eyes cloud over at the mention of my son, her head dropping into her hands. "You're too forgiving. I am begging you, please consider forgiving Dax. Try to work it out."

"I forgive him. I guess I knew as soon as I heard what was happening that he would go. That's who he is; he will go to the depths of hell to protect his family." The words are true, she sees it in my eyes, once I got past the blinding pain I knew I wasn't angry with him. I am angry with myself for setting us both up for failure.

"Does that mean . . ." The hope falls from her face as I shake my head. She stands, her face drooping with sadness. Without a word, she leaves the apartment.

Curling back into a ball, I restart the exercises and try to sleep. I know I only have a few hours until the apartment is full of my friends trying to distract me.

Music wakes me and for a moment, I'm disoriented. I'm in bed, under the covers, the sound coming from my alarm. Reaching out, I smack it off only noticing the time when I have to open one eye because I missed the button.

Bolting out of bed, I rush through my morning routine, grabbing my bag from the floor. Thankful I had the sense to set an alarm, I would have felt awful if I had missed my commitment.

I almost slam the door shut when I see that Dax is in the hall. Instead, I step into the hallway to face him.

It hurts.

My body feels like it is being torn apart, limb by limb.

Trying to ignore the way my heart stutters as he examines me closely, reacting to his sad eyes and unable to stop the physical effect his gaze has on me. "Hello, Ava."

"Hi." We stand awkwardly in the hall, a safe distance between us. The urge to grab his hand is strong, so I tuck mine in my pocket, my fists clenched at my sides. I don't know how to be around him anymore.

Unsure how to excuse myself, I'm thankful when Dax gives an excuse and goes into his apartment. My shoulders slump as I look at the shut door. Finally remembering where I was going, I race off to my car.

Noah's class surrounds me, a large piece of paper spread out in the middle of the room. Each child has their own square, their tools are their hands and feet. Several parent volunteers wait around us, ready to wash feet and hands.

"Okay, kiddos, is everyone ready to paint their square?" A chorus of excited confirmations fill the room. "Go!"

When Noah's teacher asked me to lead an art activity, I immediately agreed. I wanted to do something unique, something that enables the kids to unleash their creativity. It took some convincing the principal and the teacher needed to get parental permission, but thankfully, everyone was on board.

Screaming laughter surrounds us as we watch the kids cover their squares with blends of paint. The joy of being a child is that there are no inhibitions, no need to be perfect. They only want to have fun and paint.

Slowly the canvas fills as one by one the kids finish their squares. The patchwork of color is stunning, the mixture of colors with the hand and foot shaped presses.

"Wow. This looks amazing! When it dries, we're going to hang it in the hall with all of the children's names written around the edges." Mrs. Lehman smiles warmly at me as she hands me a thank you card. "Noah was so excited, telling his classmates how awesome you are at painting. He says you're the best artist in the world."

My eyes find Noah chatting with his friends and I smile as I watch him gesture proudly at his square. Mrs. Lehman walks away, calling attention to the class. Noah runs up and gives me a big bear hug before finding his seat.

Watching for a moment as the class gets settled, the painting laying in the center of the room drying, I feel genuinely happy. Whenever I'm with Noah, I forget about the heartache, the pain of breaking up with Dax. This feeling, this reality is why I made that choice and watching Noah, I know I will be okay.

Dax

I'M DRUNK.

I've been drunk since I finished off a case of beer within an hour of seeing Ava in the hall. The shadows under her eyes haunt me as I grabbed the first beer, by the twelfth it is worse, and rather than finding the numbness I hoped for, my brain decides it is time to be honest with myself.

I became what I tried so hard not to become: unworthy.

"Gross, it smells like a brewery in here." Andie tosses her bag in the middle of the floor, grabbing the empty bottles off the coffee table and removing the half-empty bottle from my hand. I'm too drunk to resist.

The clatter of glass as she tosses them into the garbage makes me flinch. I'm obviously not drunk enough, maybe buzzed is a better word. My eyes trail her as she comes back into the living room. I haven't seen my sister look this pissed off in a long time. "Nugget . . ."

"Don't *Nugget* me. I am so angry with you, my vision is actually blurring." She faces me straight on, if it were possible, steam would be coming from her ears. "Let's not even touch on the fact you broke Ava's heart, the girl you proposed to not even a week before. Let's focus on the fact you went into a gang house while you're on probation. Let's focus on the fact that you let Ivan manipulate you into doing something you said you would never do. Let's focus on the fact that you broke promises not only to your friends, family, and fiancée, but to yourself as well."

Her words fire straight into my heart, the fuzziness of my brain clearing as I drink the glass of water I didn't even see her set on the table. "I know."

"Dax, I love you. You're my brother, and I've spent so much time defending your actions. This is one time I can't defend. I want to be able to say to Ava that she shouldn't have ended things that she should have trusted you to know. But I can't. You made a choice, and you chose wrong." She takes a deep breath, closing her eyes as though seeing me in this state is more than she can bear. When she opens them, they've lost some of their fire. "Please tell me this was a one-time lapse."

"I'm pretty sure Ivan's broken nose will prevent him from contacting me again. That and the threat of revealing information to any source that will make his life hell, including my parole officer." She smiles when I mention breaking Ivan's nose.

"Good. Now, what are you going to do? Are you going to sit around moping? Or are you going to do something to change the way you feel?" Andie stands, not even waiting for me to answer. "You should shower. You stink."

Laughing, I heave myself off the couch. Grabbing a slice of cold pizza from the fridge, I start to sober up. She's right; I can't let one mistake take me down. Regardless of whether time will show Ava that I won't mess up again, I need to do this.

A hot shower helps me feel like I've washed the blood off of my hands. Unleashing that part of me felt disgustingly good, but I think it's because I finally turned on Ivan. I hate that part of me, the angry punk he always manipulated. I clung to that part of my life without even realizing it and the loss of a future I dreamed of was the ice-cold awakening I needed.

Picking up my phone, I do something I should have done a year ago. I block and delete Ivan's contact from my phone. That one action starts an avalanche as I cleanse my phone of any trace of that part of my life. Gone, but not forgotten. I've finally truly learned from my mistakes.

A little too late.

Later that day, I stand outside my last stop. Perry's Ink. It looks sketchy, like if I touch anything I will contract an STD, but once I step inside I'm blown away. It's edgy and more importantly, clean. Walking up to the reception desk, I'm greeted by a woman who looks like a fifties pin-up model. Her platinum blonde hair falls in waves past her shoulders, accentuating the curve of her breasts.

Popping her gum, she smiles coyly at me. "May I help you?"

Ignoring the way she licks her lower lip, I remind myself to tell Carter he should come here. She's exactly his type. My type is at home with paint on her nails, hair probably knotted at the top of her head as she creates a masterpiece. "Yeah, I have an appointment with Vic. Dax Burke."

She silently leads me into a sterile room where a heavily tattooed man sits reading. He looks up as she shuts the door behind her, shutting his book with an emphatic thud. He gets right down to business. "Here is the design, look it over and if you approve, sign the consent form on the clipboard."

He hands me a folded sheet of paper, as though he quickly scribbled something down during his break. When I unfold it, my breath is taken away. It's small, simple, shaded perfectly and conveys exactly what I want it to. Signing the consent, I remove my shirt and lay on my back watching as he preps the gun and my skin for the tattoo.

Six hours later, I'm home and exhausted.

"Where have you been?" Andie sits up from where she is reclined against Lucas. I haven't seen him since Ava ended things and I wish I could say something to fix the stare he's giving me. "You got your hair cut."

"I just cleaned it up. I was at risk of looking like I was imitating Bieber. I went and got a tattoo."

Her eyes bug out of her head. "You know they don't recommend doing that when you're feeling emotionally unstable."

"I'm perfectly stable. What you said this afternoon clicked." Lifting my shirt over my head, I expose my new ink. My only

ink.

Andie gasps as she sees it, Lucas's eyes widening before his eyes dart to mine. He gives me a silent nod, and I breathe a sigh of relief; I know I'm one step closer to fixing my fuck up.

CHAPTER 19

Ava

GIVING MY MOM a hug, I head to Joe's waiting car. Tossing my bag inside, I smile at Joe. "Hi."

He smiles back, shifting his car into gear. "You're looking better."

"I am? Good, I've gotten really good at faking it." Winking at him as I attempt to make a joke, he gives me a pity laugh. He's been surprisingly kind after Dax and I broke up, respecting me enough not to try and pick me up. It might help that he met someone at his new office. On Sunday when I dropped Noah off, he introduced me to Kate, and I really like her.

"So, I have some news." Joe keeps his eyes on the road, sending immediate warning signals through my head.

"Good news or bad news?" He grins at the skepticism in my voice.

"Mom and Dad started an education savings for Noah, that's one of the stops we're making; I'm adding you to the account so you can see what's in there. They've been so thankful that you've given us all the chance to be involved." He merges onto the highway, finally looking at me and smiling at the shock on my face.

"Wow. That's so generous." Glad that Joe and I have finally found a respectful routine, I'm grateful for that sense of normalcy in my life. I still haven't found a way to tell Noah that Dax is no longer involved in my life. Well, at least not in the way I had hoped he would be. With our circle of friends, avoiding him is near impossible.

"I wanted to let you know that I made you my beneficiary. That way if something happens to me, you don't have to worry about being able to look after Noah."

"Wow, Joe. I don't know what to say." Choking up a little, I reach over and squeeze his hand before dropping it.

"Nothing. Don't say anything. I'm his father and it's my job to make sure he's looked after."

We get through our errands quickly. We tour a couple of schools before choosing where he will go in the fall for Kindergarten.

By the time Joe drops me off at school, we're both exhausted, but I'm feeling optimistic. We spent almost an entire day together without any inappropriate comments or arguments. We got along well, and everything was Noah focused. Kate joined us for lunch and I like her even more this second time.

"Okay, well that was a productive day. I like Kate, she's good for you." Joe gets out of the car and hands me my bag.

"Does that mean you would be okay with her meeting Noah?" He looks hopeful, and I'm once again shocked at how much he has changed.

"Of course. Maybe just introduce her as your friend until you've been together for a little longer. I don't want the same issue to come up as I am having to try to figure out how to explain why Dax hasn't been around." Joe leans against the car, grimacing.

"You guys were engaged, how were you to know it would end. I see what you mean, though." Joe pushes off from the car and gives me a hug.

"Thanks for understanding. So I will drop Noah off on

Sunday at the normal time." Stepping away from him, I smile as we fall into what's becoming our normal routine.

"Perfect." Joe goes around the car, leaning on the door as he opens it up. "Ava, thanks for giving me the chance to prove myself, even when I didn't make it easy for you. I hope you get the sparkle back that you've lost, maybe you should think about what you need to get it back."

Shaking my head at him, I wave as he drives away. I know exactly what I need, I just don't trust him not to hurt me again. His ties to that other world will always be tethered to him, trying to pull him back. I don't know if he's capable of ever cutting them, because why wouldn't he have done so by now?

Later that day as I'm lying in bed trying to sleep, Joe's words keep turning over in my head. Every night different scenarios of how things with Dax could have gone down plays over and over in my head.

I could have gone with them, not giving him the option to leave without me.

I could have trusted that he meant what he said when he claimed it was a one-time thing.

I could have tried to reason with Peyton.

I could have called the police.

The thing is, none of those options solved the issue. Every one of them hurt one of us. But the longer I go without seeing him, talking to him, touching him . . . The more I think about Dax and what happened, the more I wish we could fix things without compromising who we are and what we need from each other.

I just don't think that's possible.

Why did it have to turn into this? Breaking my rule was the best thing that had happened to me, aside from Noah, and now I'm back to square one.

I wouldn't go back and change it though. The times we shared together, I wouldn't give them up.

Dax

WATCHING JOE COMFORT Ava stung. In fact, it more than stung. I'm pretty sure a ghost just stabbed me in the gut and is twisting the knife.

What makes it worse is, I have no right to feel that way. I brought this on myself. Andie thinks I did it subconsciously to sabotage what I had with Ava because on some level I still don't think I'm worthy of her.

Bounding up the steps two at a time, I'm in my apartment before Ava and Joe have said goodbye. Jealousy boils as I wish I were the one hearing her voice. Talking to her about her day.

The sound of their door shutting washes away the green-eyed monster.

Pacing the living room, my head spins with regret. Falling back on the couch, I force myself to change my thought pattern into a more productive way of thinking.

Ugh, Andie's psychology crap is rubbing off on me.

Just fix it. That's what I need to tell myself.

Ava doesn't believe that I'm done with the Vipers. That I haven't been able to let go of that life completely. It's time to prove myself to her, she makes me better, and the future I envisioned for us is quickly slipping away. Because I let it.

The next morning, I'm sitting in my regular seat in math. It's our last final. It's also one of my last opportunities to try to talk to her before school is out. Her caramel macchiato sits on her desk and the intensity with which I'm watching the door borders on scary. Forcing myself to relax, I load *Plants vs. Zombies* onto my phone and attempt to play. The effort is wasted, because I'm still watching the door. Giving up, I stuff my phone into my pocket and quit trying to pretend I'm not looking for her.

The room fills up. Ava is still not at her desk, in fact, she's not even in the classroom. It's not until Williams is handing out the exams that she slips into her seat, faltering as she sees the coffee on her desk.

Williams sets the exams face down, going over the instructions for the exam. Out of the corner of my eye, I see Ava reach a shaking hand for the coffee before taking a sip. Her eyes are on me, but before I can meet her gaze and silently try to convey that I'm not giving up, Williams tells us to begin, and her focus is on the exam.

Scanning the exam, I almost laugh at how simple it is, but I refrain when a quick scan of the room shows how intensely focused most people are. Stretching my legs out, I begin working through the problems. Slowly. If I can manage it, I will be handing in my exam at the exact same time as Ava.

Slowly working through each question, most of my thoughts are focused on her. Being this close to her, seeing the cute crease between her eyes as she focuses on a problem, I want to beat the shit out of myself for making such a huge mistake.

Pressing my thumbs to my temples, I try to push away the headache that always surfaces whenever I start going in these circles. What good does it do to dwell? But isn't that the joy of being human, our tendency to focus on our mistakes?

In the silent room, you can hear the tick-tock of the clock, and soon I see that half the time for the exam has passed and I'm only on the second page. Too slow. Shaking my head to clear it, I work through the questions as quickly as I can.

It's not enough. I was so caught up in berating myself, that I lost track of keeping pace with Ava. She stands, I feel her gaze on me as she picks up her coffee before handing in her test and rushing out of the room.

It takes everything I have not to slam my fist on the desk. I've fucked up again.

Less than ten minutes later I'm out the door, scouring the area to see if I can spot her. She's nowhere to be seen. Cursing loudly, I apologize to a group of girls who jump and back away from me quickly.

I can only imagine the look on my face. Carefully relaxing the muscles, I try for a neutral expression, apologizing once again.

My phone buzzes in my pocket reminding me I have missed messages. The first is from Carter, reminding me about the party at his house tonight.

The second is from Ava. A simple thank you for the coffee. Those five words give me something I didn't realize I was missing. Hope.

CHAPTER 20

Ava

THE NOISE COMING from Kensi and Nella's apartment shakes the walls as I make my way downstairs. I'm pretty sure by the end of the night the noise will have driven out any remaining students.

The floor vibrates, sending tingles up my legs. Kensi doesn't do anything small. Opening the door, the music blasts me. It's so loud, I stumble back against the noise. Kensi sees me and yanks me inside, wrapping her arm around me. "Fashionably late! A girl after my own heart."

Smiling indulgently, I disentangle myself in order to retrieve the drink Nella is trying to hand me. Before I can ask, Andie has cranked the music down to a volume that won't shatter the windows, ignoring the glare Kensi sends her way.

"Kens, let's remember that we want to hear each other talk." Following the girls into the room, we laugh as Kensi mutters something about talking being overrated when we can drink.

As we sit discussing summer plans, I discover that Nella and I both decided to sign up for a couple summer courses. Ignoring the chorus of "nerds" being yelled that has Andie and Kensi laughing uncontrollably, I try to focus on what Nella is saying.

"I wanted to get my statistics class out of the way, especially since I'm hoping to go on with my graduate studies focusing on research. They're offering it for the first time in an online format. They're setting us up with an online chat room, video courses with the prof and online power points. This way I can do it in my own time." Nella picks up a pillow and whacks Kensi in the face with it.

"We're about to have a mutiny on our hands." Andie and Kensi are giggling as they whisper to each other, the word "dare" causing Nella and me to shift away from them. "We're done, I swear."

Andie and Kensi pull out Jenga, and I'm tasked with setting it up since I only have one drink in me. Lucas and Andie are going down to visit Kensi on Vancouver Island, making Kensi's summer much less dreaded.

"Joe and his parents want to take Noah to Disneyland. They offered to take me as well, but I'm not going to go." Sticking out my tongue, I grab a block and slowly try to remove it from the tower, making weird sounds whenever the tower moves. Breathing a sigh of relief when I finally have the block out.

"Why not go?" Kensi makes a big show of shaking out her hands, asking me a question I've been wavering on since Joe mentioned it yesterday. She moves her eyes to the tower and carefully selects her block. "I mean, it's a pretty awesome opportunity."

"It is, and I'm grateful that they thought to ask, but I think it would be too confusing for Noah." The girls nod in agreement before erupting in cheers when Kensi knocks the tower over.

"Enough of this crap, let's play Truth or Dare." Kensi grumbles, Nella and I agreeing as we laugh at her.

The door opens, and Peyton sticks her head inside. "Sorry I'm late."

She sits on the floor next to me, and I lean over giving her a hug. "Kensi just lost Jenga and voted we move on to Truth or Dare."

The game starts innocently enough. First boyfriends, best kisses, worst kisses. We avoid touchy subjects and have fun. Gagging as I drink some random concoction that Kensi put together, I'm pretty sure she took a shot from every liquor bottle in her cupboard, so I forfeit choosing Dare again.

Over the course of the evening, I learned a few interesting facts about my friends.

Kensi told us about her worst break-up. She was in a relationship with her old boss when she went to Springfield. She went to see him as a surprise and she walked in on him and the head of human resources having sex on his desk.

Andie told us about how she ran into her ex a few weeks ago and when he tried to flirt with her, she was finally able to unleash all of her pent up anger. "I should be a bigger person, but damn it felt good!"

Nella quietly admitted she was attracted to someone at school, but she stopped there and refused to tell us who.

Peyton shocked all of us when she admitted she stripped for a brief time in the gang.

"Your turn! Now what should we ask Ava?" The girls lean in and start whispering. They're not very quiet about it and I freeze when Dax's name comes up.

"Ava, what would it take for you to consider trying again with Dax?" Kensi is the boldest of the girls; she doesn't even try to sugarcoat the question.

Looking at my hands as they twist in my lap, I think about how it felt seeing the cup of coffee on my desk. For a moment, it felt like nothing had changed, nothing had happened. That feeling has lingered all day, fueling my doubt that I had been rash in not trusting him. Then I remembered how much it hurt when he chose to leave, how scared I was wondering if he was okay, the bare feeling on my ring finger that only held a ring for a short time.

Lifting my chin, I finally respond. "I love Dax. Telling him we were done, handing him the ring was one of the most difficult decisions I ever had to make. It was the right one. I needed him to understand what breaking his promise meant, that I am serious about not being tied to that world in any way."

Pausing, I can see the looks of disappointment on their faces. They were hoping for a simple answer, but when I think about what I would need from him, to me it really is simple. "I'm not ruling out the possibility that things can be fixed. What I would need from him has not changed; a commitment that he is done with that world. He promised me that when we first started dating and he broke that promise. That's not something I thought he would do. Words aren't enough anymore."

"What about smashing Ivan's face into the concrete and telling him that if he ever tries to contact us again he will make his life a living hell? Does that count?" Peyton sticks a chip in her mouth, chewing as she waits for that to sink in. Her lips twitch as my jaw drops.

Words refuse to come out of my mouth as I gape at my friends. Nella and Kensi looked as shocked as I feel. I'm sure my face is comical right now.

"Wait. What? Seriously?" Words come out, fractured. My ears ring as I process what this could mean.

"Want to see the video?" Peyton loads it on her phone without waiting for an answer and soon all five of us are enthralled in watching Dax smash Ivan's face into the pavement, repeatedly. It's terrifying, but I can't look away as I manage to comprehend his words.

"Why . . ." Clearing my throat when it breaks, I try again. "Why didn't you show this to me sooner?"

"Bear took the video, and he just sent it to me yesterday. Otherwise, I would have shown it to you when I saw you last." Peyton clicks her phone off.

We sit silently, I have a feeling the girls are waiting for me to digest the information. "This makes things . . ." I search for the right word, a word to describe how I'm feeling. "Different."

Andie suggests we watch a movie, looking at me as I nod

mutely. Kensi makes popcorn and we all crowd onto their couch. I have no idea what movie we're watching. My mind is reeling from the video and what this could mean.

Why didn't Dax come to me?

It doesn't take long to answer my own question: he doesn't think I would believe him. Halfway through the movie, I excuse myself and head upstairs. The girls don't try to stop me.

It's as if I'm walking blind. I make it to my room, and I don't even remember walking up the stairs. Mindlessly, I automatically start digging around in my paints.

Dax

ONE OF THE things I like about these guys is that our parties are low key, and we end up gaming all night. It's a stress-free environment where I can let my guard down, something I appreciate even more now that I briefly stepped back into my old life.

Dean grumbles as Lucas snipes him for the third time. "Seriously? I'm about to throw a tantrum that could rival Noah's when he was two."

Lucas cringes, jokingly pleading with Dean not to go there. "Noah brought new meaning to the terrible two's, please don't make me revisit that time, I still have nightmares."

I ignore how the guys all eyeball me, knowing that's a sensitive area. They've already bitched me out about fucking it up. I'm sure if Dean had the energy, he would have tried to beat the shit out of me, and I would have let him.

Instead, I let them say their piece before informing them I was trying to find a way to fix it. I got varying degrees of skepticism, it was comforting.

Dean's character dies again, and he tosses the controller to Jaden. "I'm out. You have a go." He leans back into the armchair, texting. He grins at whatever the person is saying and once again, I'm consumed by jealousy. I had that, and I threw it away.

Standing abruptly, I pause the game. "I need some fresh air."

Jaden follows me outside, watching silently as I pace. "Dude, you need to relax."

"I know. I'm dwelling and that does no good." Sitting on the curb, I take a swig of my beer.

"Nah man, I get it. I've loved and lost before, but this isn't permanent. Let's go inside, try and kick Lucas's ass." Following him in, we pick up where we left off finally finding where Lucas is hiding.

It's close to one in the morning when Carter declares he's bored and wants to raid the girl's party. It doesn't take much convincing, and soon we're racing across the campus. Once inside the building, we creep to Kensi's door before smashing in.

The girls squeal as we come barreling in, throwing pillows at us. The first thing I notice is that Ava isn't there. The second thing, the thing that has stopped the guys in their tracks, is that all the girls are wearing these tiny little shorts and tank tops.

Carter jumps right in, settling himself onto the couch between Peyton and Nella. The shit-eating grin on his face showing just how much he is enjoying the view. Jaden settle on the ground, leaning against the couch by Peyton's feet and Lucas curls up on a mound of pillows next to Andie.

"What are we watching?" Carter presses play on the movie someone thought to pause, cringing when he realizes it's a chick flick.

Smiling, I quietly excuse myself and slip out the door.

Knocking quietly on Ava's door, I open it slightly. All the lights are out except in the hall. Despite knowing it's a bad idea, I walk quietly down the hall to where her door is open a crack. She's asleep on top of her covers. My body moves before my brain can comprehend what I'm doing and I gently cover her with the quilt at the foot of her bed. As I turn to leave, I'm stunned to see the number of paintings lining the floor along the wall.

They start out dark, stormy looking and slowly get brighter. Knowing Ava, it's telling me the progression of her mood.

Before I can force myself to leave, I glance at the date on the bottom right corner of the brightest painting, it's from today.

I wish I could take it into the light and look at the fine details I know cover the surface, but Ava mumbles in her sleep. Leaving quickly, that sliver of hope grows.

CHAPTER 21

Ava

I WAKE UP feeling more optimistic than I have in a long time. Taking my time to shower and get ready, for the first time in over a week, I feel human. Practically skipping down the steps, I shove open the door to my building and savor the fresh spring air.

Tilting my head up to soak in some sun, I'm tempted to throw my arms out and spin like Julie Andrews in *A Sound of Music*. Worried I'm about to start singing, I tuck my chin down and start walking.

I woke up this morning to a text from Dean, inviting me over for breakfast. A sure sign he is feeling more like himself. That combined with what Peyton showed me last night, I feel ready to tackle this and try to get it right this time.

Thinking back on that video, I shudder involuntarily. Seeing Dax like that, completely unleashed, it was scary. And a turn on. Wondering if that makes me sick, I decide it's more the realization that he could protect Noah and me than him beating Ivan up. Although, if I'm being honest, seeing Ivan face first in the dirt did give me a sick sense of satisfaction.

Hearing him cut those ties was what I needed, the guarantee he wouldn't be sucked back in every time they found a way to manipulate him using the people he loves.

My bubble is burst as I allow doubt to push its way in. What if he doesn't want me back? What if my lack of faith in him ruined my chance? Realizing we both broke promises that night, I straighten my shoulders and promise myself to fight, to give us a real chance.

Last night Kensi told me she thought that both Dax and I used that opportunity to ruin what we had, to sabotage it because we're both scared of fully trusting another person.

I hate to admit it, but she's right.

Dean lives on the ground floor of the apartment building furthest away from mine, but I'm walking so fast that it hardly takes me any time to reach his door. Pausing for a moment to catch my breath, I breathe deeply to calm myself down. One step at a time. I can't let myself get in over my head otherwise, I might just end up re-opening the wound.

Knocking loudly, I laugh as Dean cracks a joke about not breaking his door. He swings it open, his back greeting me as he heads into the kitchen where the smell of bacon makes my mouth water.

"What, no hug?" Stepping in next to him, I give his side a squeeze before folding myself onto one of his chairs.

Examining him carefully, I'm happy to see the shadows under his eyes look less like bruises and more like the normal shadows a typical university student would have.

"Bacon is more important than a hug and you know it." He turns off the oven, dumping the bacon onto a plate. Grabbing a piece, I drop it as the grease stings my fingers. "It's hot. I didn't realize I needed to inform you of that."

Ignoring him, I blow on the piece until I can pick it up, devouring it quickly. "Oh yum. That's amazing."

Dean grabs a couple breakfast quiches from his toaster oven, dropping one on each of our plates. "I slaved for hours selecting the right frozen quiche at the grocery store. You better appreciate my effort."

Teasing him as we eat, I miss these times with Dean. We used to have a breakfast date once a month, and it hasn't been happening lately. "I miss this."

"Me too." Dean's cell phone ringing cuts off whatever he was going to say, seeing the name on the screen he quickly answers. "Hey, Mom. What time . . ."

Dean grips the table, his face turning white. Standing quickly, I rush to his side and grip his shoulders tightly. I can hear his mom crying, my heart pounding as I think of the worst-case scenarios. Dean mumbles goodbye to his mom, hanging up as his shoulders start shaking.

He sobs uncontrollably, and I wrap him tightly in my arms. "Danny had a reaction to his treatment, he went into heart failure. They couldn't revive him . . . my brother is gone."

Holding him as tightly as I can as though that will keep him together, I silently cry for Dean and his family. Danny was an amazing kid. He played every sport he could and excelled at each of them. He always had a kind word for every single person, and never let his popular status at school take away his humility.

"I'm so sorry." The words are meaningless, but what else do you say?

Dean takes a few deep breaths, looking up at me. "I need to go to the hospital."

"I will drive you." He doesn't argue, handing me the keys to his truck. We're out the door and on the road in less than fifteen minutes.

Quickly sending Lucas a text, I drop my phone into my purse, reaching over to grab Dean's hand. I don't let go the whole drive.

"He was too young. I just don't understand why this happened to him. Life is too short to be miserable." Dean looks at me pointedly as he speaks. Squeezing his hand, I smile at him, my lips shaking as I fight more tears.

The drive blurs by, both of us lost in our thoughts. Right now, all I want is to rush home to Noah and wrap him in a hug for days. I can't even imagine the pain Dean's family is experiencing.

Parking the car, I only let go of Dean's hand long enough to exit the truck and lock it. I don't know if it's comforting him, but I need it too.

We find his parents in Danny's room. They thank me for driving Dean, wrapping the two of us in their arms. Quietly, I slip away to let them grieve as a family.

There is a seating area just outside the room; my legs barely hold me as I sit down, dropping my head into my hands. My mind cycles around how something can happen to someone as young and kind as Danny. I know illness doesn't hand-pick the people, it just doesn't seem fair.

Familiar voices draw my attention, leaning back in the chair I watch as Andie and Lucas lead the parade of our friends into the waiting area.

Stunned that they got here so quickly, I glance at the clock, shocked to see I've been sitting here for several hours. The door to Danny's hospital room has opened a few times, the doctor going in and out. It seems so cold that they have to fill out paperwork so soon after his passing.

Watching them wheel out his body broke my heart, the glimpse I saw of Dean and his family huddled together bringing fresh tears to my eyes.

Lucas sitting next to me draws me back to the present, and I look up at him, his face blurry. Andie sits on the other side of me, and the two of them wrap their arms around me. We sit silently like that for several minutes.

Dax's voice cuts through the moment as he suggests we find somewhere else to wait, not wanting to disrupt the family.

I don't fully hear what he's saying, but the moment I hear him refer to priorities I lose my shit. "Are you serious right now?"

Standing, I turn to face him, the anger on my face shocks everyone. I hear Lucas say my name softly, but I stick my hand out behind me to silence him.

206

"Did you really just speak about priorities when yours are so messed up? How dare you!" My voice shakes, inside I'm telling myself I'm not being fair. I don't care. All the feelings I wish I had yelled at him that day, all the thoughts I need to expel are coming out. I thought I was okay, I thought I could move past it, but the words spewing out of my mouth clearly have a different idea. "You told me you knew what you wanted, that you wanted to be a family with me and Noah. Yet first chance you get, you go running back like a puppet for Ivan. No thought of the consequences, no concern that you could have landed in jail, or worse, been killed. Do you have any idea what that did to me? And what about Noah? Do you honestly think he hasn't noticed you missing from our lives?"

I get right in his face, pushing him back as he stands there stunned. Every feeling of betrayal. Every feeling of abandonment comes out of me. And he doesn't say anything.

"So tough guy, you have nothing to say for yourself?" I'm trying to pick a fight, and I want him to fight back. Part of me thinks if he fights back that means he wants to fight for us. The rational side of my brain tells me I'm stupid.

Hands grip my arms, dragging me away as I realize I had been yelling. Dean stands in the open door, his brow furrowed as he watches Andie and Kensi drag me away. Peyton and Nella follow closely. Shame finally hits me as I see Dean trailing behind us.

"You can let me go. I promise to behave." The hands drop away cautiously. Leaning against the wall, I cringe as Dean stops in front of me. "I'm so sorry. I didn't realize I had so much pent up. That was completely unacceptable."

He enfolds me in his arms, whispering so only I can hear. "Ava, if you feel enough to argue with him there is still something worth fighting for. Please do something for me."

He pulls back so he can see me nod.

"Okay, you and Dax are driving home together. Just the two of you. That gives you four hours to hash everything out." He grabs my hand and drags me back to the waiting room. Pointing

between Dax and me, his next words have everyone else grinning. "You two, out. Drive home together and work this shit out."

With that, he drops my hand and goes to where his parents stand at the nurse's station. Dax walks towards the exit, not waiting to see if I'm following. Hustling to catch up, I don't look behind me.

Dax

UNLOCKING THE DOOR to my new SUV, I open the passenger door and wait for Ava to climb in. The look of shock in her eyes has me resisting a grin. I don't want to fight with her, but I know she wants to yell at me, and she wants me to yell back, so that's what I will give to her.

Holding my face firm, I watch her eyes flick between my face and the car. She brushes past me, settling into her seat as I slam the door shut. The feeling of her shoulder brushing my chest makes it hard to stick with keeping my hands off her, so I walk slowly around the back of the vehicle ensuring I have full control of myself before getting in.

Neither of us says anything as I work my way to the highway. I practically feel the words bubbling inside Ava, so I just wait.

"I'm mad at you. Do you even understand how much it hurt me when you broke your promise to me? To tell me you have no interest in going back to that world and then jump right back in with little regard for me begging you, not asking, but begging you to stay." Her words come out soft, almost detached. That hurts more than the yelling did.

"I'm mad at me too. But I'm not the only one who broke a promise. Why didn't you trust me? It wasn't just for anything; I wish you understood how hard that choice was." Keeping my voice level, I try to maintain the same tone of voice she spoke in.

This time when she speaks, her calm facade is cracked, her voice no longer detached. "I did trust you, I trusted you not to break my heart. I trusted you with my son. I trusted you to say yes when you asked me to marry you, that moment we made a silent promise to each other that we came first. You broke my trust."

As she speaks, her voice gets louder, the scratchiness of her words burn my throat, and when I respond, my words come out in a shout. "I went there for Peyton. The whole way there, you were on my mind, and when I was there, I made sure I cut the damn ties. But if the trust is gone is there any way for me to prove it to you?"

Her chest heaves as we glare at each other. Pulling over to the side of the road, I turn the car off and face her. "I know you did, I saw the damn video!"

She unbuckles her seatbelt and kneels on the seat, her ass on her heels, crossing her arms as she waits for me to respond. "Video?"

She smiles grimly as I lose steam. "Peyton's brother videotaped you smashing Ivan's face into the ground."

Closing my eyes, I dread to think about what's shown in that video. For her to see that side of me, cruel and relentless, I never wanted that to happen. "Shit."

"Why didn't you come to me? Was I so easy to let go?" The words are whispered and I finally see the real fear behind the words.

"Ava . . . No. Walking away from you was difficult, and if I thought I truly deserved you, I don't think it would have happened." Lifting my hand, I squeeze it into a fist, resisting touching her.

She stares at me silently and I cannot bear to see the war on her face as she decides what to do so I close my eyes and wait. We've said so much and still haven't said what we need to. When her voice comes again, I feel her breath on my cheek. "Dax, there is no doubt in my mind that you are it for me." Slowly opening my eyes, I lose myself in the depths of her blue eyes. "Is it completely insane that I was kind of turned on seeing you beat the shit out of him?"

Laughing softly, I lean into the hand that gently strokes my face. "Yes."

"All I needed was to hear those words and know you meant them." Her eyes close as a tear sneaks out.

Wiping it away with my thumb, I whisper to her, "I will never make the mistake of walking away from you again."

Breathing her in, I wrap my hand in her hair and close the distance between us. Pouring every ounce of fear I've felt at losing her, relief at feeling her lips on mine and the overwhelming love that I have for her into my kiss, I don't stop until we're gasping for air.

"Ava . . ." I pause, not knowing how to ask what I need to.

"It's okay. I don't think we need to talk this to death." She cringes at the word death.

"I know. I was going to ask . . . Does Noah hate me?" I haven't allowed myself to think about Noah. I didn't think I deserved to, but he's been on my mind fighting his way out.

"Ummm . . . Well, you see, I never told him we broke up." The words are out in a rush, a rare blush tinging her cheeks. "I couldn't bear it, so I made excuses for you."

"I'm going to be selfish and be relieved to hear that."

Ava moves back into her seat, buckling in and I start the car. Her hand grasps mine and it feels like a missing piece of me has found its way home.

We quickly fall back into our comfortable routine, talking about everything that's happened since we parted. The time was short, but it felt endless.

The drive passes quickly, Ava leading me silently to her room. Inside her room, I drag her over to the paintings I saw the other night. "Tell me about these."

She looks them over, her emotions flickering across her face. "The first one is from the night you left. There is one from every day after. I was in a dark place, and this was the only way to get those emotions out. I had to be present for Noah, so everything built up over the day."

"That last one, it seems happier." Pulling her against my chest, I rest my chin on her shoulder as we look at it.

"I painted that one after I decided we weren't over, at least on my side." She chuckles softly, the sound reverberating right to my core. "Not that you would have been able to tell by my outburst today."

Spinning her in my arms, I grab her ass and lift her. Groaning as her legs wrap around my hips, I walk us over to the bed. Lowering her down, I bury my face in her neck sucking the sensitive spot below her ear. "That's how I knew we could work this out. There was fight back in your body."

Growling as her hands find their favorite spot in my hair, my fingers grip her hip with bruising force. "I need you. Hard, fast, and fucking rough."

Wasting no time, we shed our clothes. Yanking her off the bed, I bend her over the bed and bury myself in her pussy. Clamping my hands on her hips, I groan as she fists the sheets in her hands and shoves her hips back into me.

Pounding into her forcefully, I grab a fistful of hair and pull her back into my chest. The new angle brings her to climax, my release pulsing through me as she clenches around me.

We collapse onto the bed, sweat glistening over our skin. Ava turns in my arms, her breath catching in her throat as she sees my tattoo for the first time.

CHAPTER 22

Ava

UNABLE TO TAKE my eyes off Dax's tattoo, I trace it lightly with my fingers. The silhouette of three people holding hands is subtle and beautiful. My legs are entwined with his, I don't want one inch of us not to be touching.

Rolling onto him, I run my fingers through his hair, tugging gently. He kisses the palm of my hand before grabbing my hips and flipping me onto my back. Grinning knowingly as he reaches for his jeans, I run my nails down his spine eagerly.

Dax rolls away from me, pulling me up to a sitting position in one smooth motion. He kneels in front on me, and I finally focus on what's in his hand. "Ava, I've seen what it would be like to lose you, I never want to go through that again. Please say you'll marry me . . . again."

"Of course I will." He slides the ring onto my finger, wrapping his arms tightly around me.

"I love you."

"I love you too." I could stay in this moment forever, but the time catches my eye and I grin ruefully at him. "We need to go."

An hour later and we're at my parent's house, Noah's arms wrapped around Dax's waist. "Mister Dax! I've missed you."

The No Bad Boy Rule

"I missed you too, Noah." He crouches down, hugging Noah. I barely hear the words as he whispers them. "I'm sorry I've been gone."

"Noah, we have something to tell you. Mister Dax and I are getting married." Noah looks between us, a wide grin on his face.

"Does that mean I can call you Dad?" He looks to Dax, who looks at me. Smirking, I just stare back letting him make that call.

"Of course." There is a catch in Dax's throat, reaching over I squeeze his hand.

"Let's go celebrate. I think we need to get a banana split." Noah quickly shoves on his shoes, grabbing each of our hands as we leave the house together.

Dax looks at me over Noah's head, his eyes shining. I know the look is reflected on my face. Turns out loving a bad boy isn't such a terrible idea.

They're my perfect family.

THE end

ACKNOWLEDGEMENTS

It's hard to believe I'm writing acknowledgments for the third time, it never gets any easier.

Most importantly, I want to thank you for picking up this book and reading it. Every time someone contacts me to tell me how much they loved my characters is something I cherish.

This book has been wonderfully challenging. Dax and Ava had a mind of their own, straying from what I had initially planned for their story. Their love is fast, furious and all consuming, but for them it worked. While I was writing, I spoke with a few people about their own love stories and I discovered that there is no real timeline. My parents were married within a year of dating. Aaron knew he loved me the night we met and here we are almost 13 years later. It was after this realization that I decided to stop fighting the way the words were flowing and roll with it.

Now it's time to thanks to everyone who helped make The No Bad Boy Rule what it is.

Thank you Eric and Bryant for combining your amazing talents for this phenomenal cover. I couldn't have asked for a better image for this book.

Kari, you always make my covers beautiful. Thank you for letting me email you ten times in a row as different thoughts cross my mind and rolling with it.

Thank you Tami for making the inside as beautiful as the outside. You're quick, professional and absolutely delightful to work with.

Thank you Jessica for your encouragement and support.

Thank you for loving these characters as much as I do and thank you for doing such a phenomenal job editing.

Thank you Missy for joining my editing team and for pushing me to be the best writer I can be. Your feedback has been incredibly valuable and I can't wait to continue to grow and improve.

I couldn't have done this without the support of Aaron specifically. He never ceases to amaze me in how kind and generous he is. I get a little tunnel vision toward the end of a book and he rolls with all of my crazy requests.

Lori and Kristi, I really have no words to express how much the two of you mean to me. You're there every step of the way and I love you both.

I'm so blessed to have amazing author friends to encourage me and support me through this journey. Thank you so much to Fabiola Francisco, Stacy Borel and Alicia Rae. Whether we sprinted or just talked, I know I can always count on you to be there for me.

A very special thank you to the blogs who have helped spread the word about me and supported my books. I truly cannot express enough gratitude for everything you do.